WITCH QUEEN BOOK FOUR

MIDNIGHT WITCH

A.D. STARRLING

COPYRIGHT

DISCOVER AD STARRLING'S SEVENTEEN UNIVERSE AND MORE

Seventeen Series

OTHER SERIES BASED IN THE SEVENTEEN UNIVERSE
Legion
Witch Queen

MILITARY ROMANTIC SUSPENSE
Division Eight

MISCELLANEOUS
Void - A Sci-fi Horror Short Story
The Other Side of the Wall - A Horror Short Story

Mae Jin's ribcage shuddered violently where she lay face down in the freezing rain. The shallow puddles forming under her broken and battered body leached away what little warmth remained in her bones, leaving her veins filled with ice and her throat choked with fear.

"No."

The denial fell from her lips in a tortured whisper. The sound was lost in the clap of thunder that tore across the distant, angry sky.

Her ears rang, adding to the dizziness making the world spin around her. Nausea churned her belly when she attempted to lift her head. She blinked and bit her lip hard, anger overriding the dark despair that threatened to rob her of hope.

Fire flared within her as she reached for her magic.

Don't, my witch.

Mae's breath caught at the wretched plea. Tendons screamed in her neck as she turned her head.

Brimstone lay a few feet to her left. His bright eyes and rich fur were dulled by the attacks they had sustained and his chest quivered with his shallow panting. Hellreaver gleamed flatly next to him, voices silent and ragged blade motionless where he poked out from under a pile of rubble.

Mae clenched her jaw. *This isn't happening! Where did we go wrong?!*

Her nails scored the cracked tiles as she garnered the last of her strength and pushed up onto her hands and knees, her limbs trembling so hard that she knew she would soon be unable to move. Hotness drenched her abdomen and thigh, blood surging anew from her wounds.

"Stand down, demon," someone said coldly.

Goosebumps prickled her skin at the voice. It took all her willpower to raise her head and meet the gaze of the man who had spoken.

He glared at her, his mouth a thin line and his eyes and those of his familiar gleaming with distaste. A dark portal distorted the air behind them. It framed the others at his side, the blood-red light of the Harvest Moon adding another layer of menace to their daunting presence where it pierced the turbulent clouds visible through the broken church roof.

A woman laid a hand upon his arm. "Come. It is time for us to leave."

Fury and anguish curdled Mae's stomach in equal measure at the possessive look she gave the man. He nodded curtly, cast a dismissive glance at Mae, and turned to enter the rift.

The tears blurring Mae's vision spilled onto her cheeks. "Don't."

His shoulders tightened at her low mumble. For a moment, she thought her voice had finally reached him.

The hate that set his pupils aglow when he looked at her shattered whatever slim hope she still clung to.

"You try my patience, demon. Be thankful they asked me to spare you." His gaze swept the figures waiting for him before landing on her once more. "The next time we meet, I will not be as forgiving."

Blood pounded dully in Mae's skull as she watched them disappear inside the rift, disbelief a living thing twisting her insides.

"Don't go!" she begged brokenly.

The portal closed with a hiss of corruption that seemed to mock her.

Mae stared blindly at the spot where the man had vanished, the agony twisting her heart so fierce she almost wished it would strike her dead.

A scrambling sound came from behind her. Someone climbed the wreckage of broken masonry and wood that was all that remained of the nave and stumbled unsteadily toward her.

"Mae!"

A man dropped at her side, his body casting ripples in the growing puddles.

Strong arms closed around her. She was pulled up into a solid embrace. Mae sagged as his warmth cocooned her, her fingers digging into his flesh where he cradled her to his chest. His familiar nudged Brimstone and Hellreaver with a worried sound.

A strangled sob left her then, her throat so tight and hot she struggled to draw air.

"It's okay," the man whispered in a harrowed tone. "It's going to be okay."

His trembling voice finally unlocked the scream building up inside her. Mae lifted her face to the stormy sky and bellowed out her rage and loss.

ONE WEEK AGO

"Four giant meatball subs and two pastrami cheesesteaks with extra bacon!"

Mae brightened. "Here."

She slipped through the crowd, took her order from the deli guy, and made for the exit.

Those smell nice, Brimstone rumbled, trotting beside her. He licked his chops. *I approve of the chef's new meatball recipe.*

A whine came from the pendant on her chest.

I wanted three meatball subs, Hellreaver protested. *Two sandwiches are not gonna cut it, my witch.*

"Consider it a diet," Mae grunted.

Hellreaver sucked in air. *Wait. Are you saying I've—I've gained weight?!*

Mae pursed her lips at the demonic weapon. "You've definitely grown...chunkier in the last month. Those fiends of yours are nothing but gluttons. I mean, granted demons have a high metabolic rate, but you guys seriously need to cut back on the carbs."

Hellreaver vibrated with horror before promptly going into a sulk. Brimstone wheezed, eyes crinkling and not an ounce of sympathy on show.

An autumnal wind sent dead leaves dancing around Mae's legs as she crossed the road to Grandview General. She entered the main building of the hospital and nodded and smiled at the staff who greeted her while she navigated the busy corridors. Even though it had been over three months since Grandview was attacked by the Dark Council, many still considered her their hero.

Having the people whose lives she'd saved treat her with god-like deference had made Mae feel awkward at first. When she'd realized there was little she could do about it, she'd decided to go with the flow. She swallowed a sigh as she took the elevator to the tenth floor.

At least they aren't as bad as the sorcerers and witches who keep wanting to meet with me.

Her popularity had soared since her first official appearance as the Witch Queen in Philadelphia and covens were now lining up to try to get into her good graces.

It is only right that they swear their loyalty to you, Brimstone said with a haughty sniff. *You are their queen, after all.*

"You know how I feel about people kowtowing to me." Mae shuddered as she headed for the emergency stairwell. "It gives me the heebie-jeebies."

She stepped out onto the rooftop of the building, navigated the banks of elevator shafts and air vents spewing out steam until she reached her favorite spot overlooking the river, and plopped down on the ground. She gazed out over the estuary and the distant boroughs of Brooklyn and Queens as she took the sandwiches out of their bags, one eye on the storm clouds racing across the horizon to the east.

"Looks like we're gonna have more rain tonight."

Brimstone grunted around his meatball sub. *I like it. There's no rain in Hell. Even the kingdom Azazel created on Earth suffered from a lack of it due to his demonic influence.* He lifted his head and sniffed the air. *He ended up creating artificial clouds in the end. It was as much for the benefit of his people as it was for Ran Soyun, who came from a rich and verdant land.*

Mae's heart lurched at the mention of the father and mother she had never known. A month had passed since she had sensed Ran Soyun and seen Azazel, deep within the magic nexus beneath Prague. Though it had been her first meeting with the fallen angel who had gifted humankind with his ungodly powers, Na Ri, the soul whose reincarnation she embodied, had trembled with joy and love upon seeing their father. It was Azazel who had taught them the spell they needed to curb the devastating Hellfire Magic that had been unleashed upon the city. And it was Ran Soyun's magic that had healed her and Nikolai's drained cores after they'd achieved that near impossible feat.

Mae hugged her knees to her chest. "Tell me more."

Brimstone pressed his flank against her side and

started talking. The random tales he told her offered a peek into how life had been in the realm Azazel had created for his wife and those loyal to them. Hellreaver stopped pouting and added details and anecdotes from when he and Brimstone had lived with Azazel in the Underworld.

It had become their habit as of late. Mae loved nothing more than listening to them talk about the humans, demons, and hellbeasts she had never known, and Na Ri's short and happy life among them before her untimely death.

She was unwrapping her second pastrami sandwich when her cell phone buzzed with an incoming message. It was Roman Volkov.

Training sucks SO hard.

Mae smiled. She could imagine the teenager's heartfelt sigh as he'd typed the text.

A sorcerer born to one of the most powerful families of magic users in existence, Roman was a distant cousin of Vlad Vissarion and had inherited the devastating Fire Magic a select few sorcerers and witches in the Vissarion bloodline exhibited. The last Vissarion to own that power had been Katarina Vissarion, Vlad's mother.

It was from the knowledge she'd passed on in her journal that Roman had learned how to wield his Fire Magic in secret. Unbeknownst to him, his abilities had ended up placing him in the line of sight of Oscar Beneventi and the Dark Council.

Nikolai Stanisic's trip to Prague toward the end of summer had been cut short when he, Mae, and Vlad had been forced to face the Dark Council alongside their allies. It had been a deadly confrontation that had seen the white magic sorcerer gain new powers and Roman freed from Oscar and Barquiel's grasp before they could use the young man for their nefarious scheme.

The Dark Council had never suspected the secret Roman had been keeping from everyone. Like Nikolai, he too could access ley lines, making them the only two sorcerers in the world with that gift. But it left him and his chameleon familiar Filomena with the same debilitating side effects that Nikolai suffered from.

Just as Nikolai and his familiar Alastair had gone to Prague to train with the Council of the Moon to learn how to overcome this weakness, so too had Roman and Filomena. Since the closest thing to his Fire Magic was Sun Magic, they had traveled to Egypt to train with Nadia Hadid and the Council of the Sun after his school term finished in Prague.

It was the agreement Bryony Cross, Ludmila Vissarion, and Budimir Volkov had collectively come to a few weeks ago.

Mae smiled wryly. It hadn't been difficult to convince Nadia to take on the task. She and her council had as much to gain from training Roman as he had from working with them.

CHAPTER TWO

MAE MESSAGED ROMAN BACK.

It can't be that bad.

His reply had her smiling.

Filo and I are planning on running away. We're thinking of bribing a camel rider.

Mae raised an eyebrow as she tapped out a response.

A camel rider? Where the heck are you? I thought you were training in Cairo!

We're in a fortress in the desert. There are enough guards in this place to rival Fort Knox.

Mae grimaced. Considering what had happened to

the headquarters of the Council of the Moon during their last battle with the Dark Council, she could hardly blame Nadia and her coven for taking extra precautions. Marlena Kosek, Nikolai's aunt and the High Priestess of the Prague coven, had only just found a new location to replace the one that had been destroyed at the end of summer.

I have to go. My jailor calls.

Mae chuckled.

Say hi to Nadia for me.

Will do. See you soon.

Mae had promised Roman he and Filomena could visit her in New York for a short vacation once they'd finished their training in Egypt. She still hadn't told Nikolai and Vlad about this.

She chewed her lip. *No doubt they'll have something to say about that.*

Brimstone finished wolfing down his second meatball sub and gave her a side-eyed look. *You know you're only giving that boy false hope by letting him think he has a chance of becoming your consort.*

Mae met the fox's shrewd gaze. "I know. But I want to support him."

Roman had expressed his wish to be considered for the role of her future partner when he'd come to New York with Budimir and Ludmila a few weeks back.

She sighed. "I mean, why do I even need a consort in the first place?"

In your case, it would be best if you had one. Brimstone grunted. *Or several, in fact. That sorcerer is lucky you haven't jumped him yet.*

Mae couldn't deny this. Living under the same roof as Nikolai was becoming a dangerous exercise in self-control, never mind what Vlad did to her libido whenever he was around.

I don't see what the problem is with taking them all as your consorts, my witch, Hellreaver stated. *Orgies are not to be underestimated.*

Mae's cell started ringing before she could come up with a suitable riposte. It was Bryony Cross this time.

"Hi, Bryony. What's up?"

"There's a reception this Friday I would like you to attend," the New York coven High Priestess announced without preamble.

Mae swallowed a groan. "Why?"

Bryony ignored her sullen tone. "Representatives from our South American sister covens wish to pay their respects to you." She paused, her tone turning sharp. "Your little friend Cortes will be in attendance. Did you know he's joined the Medellin coven and is next in line to be their High Priest?"

Mae's eyebrows shot up. "No, I didn't."

Enrique Cortes was the second-in-command and *de facto* future head of the *Bacatá Cartel,* one of the most dangerous gangs in South America. Had it not been for an ugly twist of fate, Cortes would have grown to be a powerful sorcerer instead of a criminal. Born into a prestigious but cruel family of rare Arcane Magic users, he was cast out of the world of magic after his familiar was killed and his core broken when he was only a teenager.

It was his aunt who had struck the blows that had rendered him unable to use his powers. Threatened by his genius potential and keen to assume the mantle of leadership she felt she was owed, Raya Medeiros had had no qualms squashing the young sorcerer related to her by blood. Ironically, she had never become the High Priestess of the Medellin coven. Instead, she'd joined ranks with the Sorcerer King and taken on the role of his most valuable seer.

Cortes had finally gotten his revenge in Prague by killing Raya and her familiar during their battle with the Dark Council. It was a feat that had no doubt made the Sorcerer King furious and put a target on his back.

"And he only started using his magic properly at the end of summer," Mae mumbled, suitably impressed. Cortes's expression after he'd killed Raya flashed before her eyes. She wrinkled her nose, wary. "He didn't get rid of anyone who was being considered for that role, right?"

Bryony sighed. "I wish I could claim that, but no. He is just that strong. The Medellin coven had no option but to welcome him into their fold. I heard rumors he challenged their most powerful members to a combined duel and totally trashed them."

A warm feeling blossomed in Mae's chest. She was glad she and Nikolai had managed to repair Cortes's broken core. He was someone she knew she could count on to help her defeat the Sorcerer King, regardless of his criminal affiliations. He'd helped them find Roman after all.

"Are you smiling right now?" Bryony said suspiciously.

"No," Mae said guiltily. She hesitated. "So, does this mean Enrique has finally reconciled with his family?"

When she'd last spoken to him, Cortes had intimated he would have to make contact with the kin who had abandoned him if he wished to officially re-enter the world of magic and be recognized as a sorcerer.

"Reconciled is not quite the right word." Bryony sighed. "He pretty much subjugated them into acknowledging him as their head. Between you and me, that family totally deserves their fate."

Mae scratched her cheek awkwardly. "Ah."

She couldn't exactly blame Cortes. It wasn't as if she hadn't done some subjugation herself in Philadelphia. Her first Annual Grand Meeting had begun and ended somewhat explosively.

Brimstone huffed. *That was different. Those fools needed to learn some humility.*

Mae was distracted by Bryony's voice.

"Honestly, it scares me how many criminal organization heads you've got twisted around your little finger," the witch continued sourly. "First Yuliy Vissarion, then Budimir Volkov, and now Cortes. Your mother worries about you."

"It's not as if I'm doing it on purpose," Mae

protested. She paused as Bryony's words sank in. "Wait. You and Yoo-Mi talk?"

"She comes over for tea sometimes."

Mae shuddered. The thought of her first-generation South Korean matriarch mother indulging in small talk with one of the most powerful witches on the East Coast was enough to give her heartburn.

"The party is in the Élysée Room, at Chateau Monteville. I'll have Abraham send you the details. Nikolai's also invited, of course." Bryony sniffed. "Don't be late."

CHAPTER THREE

Nikolai's face took on the expression of a man who'd just been informed he had a venereal disease when Mae told him about the party over dinner that night.

"Another one?" He stabbed his steak forcefully with his fork, sliced off a chunk of meat with barely suppressed irritation, and stuffed it vengefully in his mouth. "How about she sticks us in a zoo and be done with it?"

Alastair rustled his feathers with obvious displeasure where he was eating a bowl of nuts and raisins on the windowsill, his emotions attuned to his sorcerer's mood.

"Yeah, well, I'm not happy about it either." Mae grimaced. "I don't think a pantsuit is gonna cut it this time."

Nikolai made a sympathetic noise while he chewed and swallowed.

After news of how they'd faced down the Dark

Council in Philadelphia and Prague had started circulating in the magic community, numerous overseas covens had started getting in touch with Bryony to arrange introductions to their Witch Queen. Word of Nikolai's abilities had also reached their ears, which meant everyone now wanted to get into the good graces of the only white magic sorcerer who could access ley lines, regardless of his past association with the Dark Council. Add to this the rumor that he was a contender for the position of her consort and the sorcerer was practically having to beat off the sudden interest in his person.

Mae frowned. *It's a good thing we kept the fact that Roman can also access ley lines a secret.*

The sharp faces of the Vissarion matriarch and Roman's grandfather rose before her. She couldn't even contemplate the level of trouble she'd be in if that slipped out.

The number of people who give me acid indigestion keeps on growing.

The matter at hand had her furrowing her brow once more. This was going to be their third official social event in as many weeks.

Now that they'd learned the Dark Council had somehow gotten their hands on the *Book of Shadows*, work on fixing the skeleton key that could open up the *Book of Light* had stalled. With no sign of impending funny business from their enemy, Mae and Nikolai had had no option but to begrudgingly accede to Bryony's requests to meet with other covens in what everyone knew would be a brief period of peace. They were both acutely aware that the war with the Dark Council would not be won with their powers alone. They needed allies and the fastest way to grow their supporters was by mingling with them.

They could just about tolerate coven politics and the humdrum of having to engage in small talk with people they didn't know. It was the fact that they had to wear monkey suits for the occasions that annoyed them the most.

"Maybe you should ask Vlad if you can check out his wardrobe," Mae suggested.

Nikolai scowled. "I'd rather poke myself in the eye. Besides, I can afford to buy my own suits." He appraised her over his wine glass. "You gonna get a new dress?"

Mae's pulse quickened a little at his heated gaze. She did her best not to squirm in her chair as she considered her answer. "I, er, have one already."

Nikolai stiffened. Hellfire Magic flashed briefly in his pupils.

Uh-oh, Brimstone said conversationally between bites of pizza. *He's pissed.*

Hellreaver sniggered around his steak. *She likes them hot and brooding.*

Mae flashed a jaundiced look at the weapon.

"That bastard got you another dress?" Nikolai ground out.

"He got me two, actually," Mae confessed, avoiding his gaze.

Nikolai's knuckles whitened on the stem of his

glass. "They'd better not be like that contraption he gifted you in Philadelphia."

Mae swallowed. The dress Vlad had gotten her for the reception of the Annual Grand Meeting had been positively illegal. She was glad she'd never shown Nikolai the lingerie that went with the outfit. She bit her lip.

The thought of showing any kind of underwear to the sorcerer had her cheeks warming.

Nikolai misinterpreted her blush. Heat distorted the air around him, the aura of Hellfire Magic barely suppressed.

"They are, aren't they?" he said between gritted teeth.

Mae eyed the smoke detector in the ceiling. "How about you calm down before you set that off?"

A fire alarm started blaring through the building. They both jumped.

Nikolai furrowed his brow. "That wasn't me."

Brimstone's ears cocked to and fro. A growl rumbled up his throat as he rose to his feet. *My witch.*

Mae stiffened at his warning. She'd just sensed what he'd detected.

"That's coming from beneath us!"

Nikolai's eyes widened when he picked up on the anomaly.

They were out the front door in seconds, their familiars at their side and Hellreaver in Mae's hand. Mae reached for her magic as they raced down the stairs.

Nullify!

The wordless incantation returned nothing. She clenched her jaw. This wasn't the work of Dark Council sorcerers and witches.

It was raining heavily when they emerged on the street.

Mae's stomach dropped.

People were screaming and running out of the main entrance of the old movie theater beneath the apartment. A sour taste filled her mouth when she saw the lacerations a few sported.

She recognized the stench exuding from their wounds.

Frustration churned her belly. *Why couldn't I sense anything until a minute ago?!*

Crimson magic lit Brimstone's eyes and radiated from his fur. *They must have come through a portal.*

Tension thrummed through Mae as she unleashed a muted version of *Wind Fury*. The spell cleared a path for her and Nikolai so they could make their way inside the dark building, the panicked crowd gasping and crying out in surprise as they were gently moved aside by an invisible force.

The throng of people escaping the movie house thinned as they aimed for the source of the irregularity, the emergency lights flickering above them adding to the eerie undercurrent drenching the interior.

The cinema housed five theaters.

They found the cause of the disturbance in the second largest one.

CHAPTER FOUR

Sulfur teased Mae's nostrils as she and Nikolai entered the murky space. A classic black and white horror movie from the 1930s was playing on the screen to their right. The light cast macabre shadows upon the stage and the rows of empty seats at the front of the auditorium. Sinister growls sent shivers skittering down her spine as her vision adjusted to the gloom. Brimstone's hackles rose.

Mae's pulse stuttered as she followed the demonic fox's gaze to the rear of the theater.

A group of college-age kids huddled in on themselves where they were surrounded by a horde of grotesque monsters in the second to last row.

The creatures were as black as night and stood some three feet tall. A foul, red light radiated from their pupils. Corruption writhed in the air in oily strands that coiled around their misshapen heads and crooked bodies. Some had two heads and were covered in fur and scales, while others bore quills and tusks.

Mae didn't have to be a genius to know they were not of earthly origin.

She clenched her teeth. "Brim, what are those?"

Heat warmed her core as Brimstone's powers swelled. He shook himself out and transformed into his nine-tailed demon form.

"They are hellbeasts." He raised his head and sniffed the air, his eyes glinting with menace. "A portal to Hell opened here recently."

Man, I haven't seen hellboars in ages, Hellreaver said wistfully.

"Wait," Mae said leadenly. "Those are hellboars?!" She pointed an accusing finger at the quilled creatures. "I thought you said they were the best things to eat in Hell!"

They are, once you get rid of their spines, the weapon protested.

Nikolai unleashed his spear. He eyed the drool oozing from Hellreaver's blades with a grimace. "Let me guess. He wants them for dinner."

Alastair clucked disapprovingly on his shoulder.

"He can't. He's on a diet."

Hellreaver whined petulantly at Mae's steadfast tone.

The demonic beasts whirled around at the sound. Their growls intensified when they saw Brimstone's towering figure. The light of Hell flared in their obsidian eyes.

Magic flooded Mae's veins. She stretched out a hand and barked out a defensive spell. "*Shield!*"

A red sphere made of runes bloomed around the

college students. They cried out and pressed closer to one another, faces ashen with terror. The hellbeasts snarled and twisted around. They attacked the barrier with their claws and fangs, to no avail.

"You're not getting through that, assholes," Mae said with a fierce smile.

The monsters shuddered as they turned. They grew another foot.

Mae's smile faded. "I didn't know they could do that."

Nikolai shook his head and sighed. "You just had to piss them off, didn't you?"

The monsters roared and bounded toward them at an impossible speed, their deformed figures blurring with shadows as they leapt the rows of seats.

Moon Magic and white magic flared in Nikolai's eyes. "Dammit! They're fast!"

The bond that bound Mae to Brimstone and Hellreaver brightened inside her as she called upon the demon magic that lived in her core. Hellreaver shot out of her hand and sliced a heavy cut into the face of the hellwolf approaching her with gaping maws. The monster screeched and dropped to the ground as his serrated blades chomped into its flesh.

Nikolai blasted two hellboars with dazzling spell bombs. He cursed as the monsters released a volley of barbed quills. Hellfire Magic burst forth from his fingers. The inky crimson washed across the theater interior, obliterating the deadly spines and the beasts who had released them.

The front row seats and the curtains on the stage caught fire.

The sprinklers came on. Steam fizzed on Alastair's fiery wings.

Nikolai caught Mae's stare. She had gripped a two-headed hellhound in a headlock and was keeping a hellwolf from tearing into her by pressing her foot down on its neck.

He shrugged. "What?"

Mae rolled her eyes, punched the hellhound in the snouts, and picked up the hellwolf with *Wind Fury*.

Brimstone's tails vibrated with power as he fended off the monsters attacking him, his giant paws sending them crashing into the walls with high-pitched whines. Hellreaver chomped and sliced his merry way through their enemy as he zoomed around the theater with evil cackles.

It took less than ten minutes for them to dispose of the monsters. By then, the college kids inside Mae's shield had all fainted from shock.

A man with a gun and a scowl barged inside the theater just as Nikolai removed his spear from the eye of the last hellwolf. Jared Dickson slowed when he saw the dead monsters.

"The hell?" the Immortal muttered.

Mae looked past the NYPD detective. "You came alone?"

"I told the other officers to stay outside." Jared put away his gun and fixed her with a sour stare. "Seeing as this was your place, I gathered it wouldn't be your run-of-the-mill incident."

Mae narrowed her eyes. "I really don't like how you make it sound like this is all my fault."

Jared ignored her accusation and stopped beside them. Lines furrowed his brow as he studied the hellbeasts.

He prodded one with his shoe. "This the Dark Council's work?"

"I have no idea." Mae ran a hand through her hair and grimaced when it came away soaking wet. "They came through a portal. Luckily, it doesn't look like they killed anyone." She indicated her shield. "There are some kids back there who got trapped."

Jared started up the aisle. "They hurt?"

"I don't think so."

Mae and Nikolai followed the Immortal. Mae frowned when she noticed the cut on the sorcerer's arm.

"It'll soon heal," Nikolai said lightly at her expression.

Jared eyed the charred remains of the seats and curtains he'd set alight. "What'd you guys do, try to burn the place down?"

Nikolai avoided his accusing gaze. "It was an accident."

"Sure it was." Jared looked over at Mae. "How about you turn off the sprinklers? This water is erasing all the evidence."

"How about we wait for the fire department to do that?" Mae suggested coolly.

"It'll be faster if you do it," Jared insisted.

Mae pursed her lips. "I'm just a tool to you, aren't I?"

She cast a wave of magic at the ceiling. Metal screamed. The sprinklers imploded. A pipe burst and released a high-pressure jet that smashed the window of the projection room.

Jared and Nikolai leveled dull stares at her.

"Told you we should have waited for the fire department," she said smugly.

My witch, Brimstone warned.

Mae whirled around. She stiffened.

Jared's eyes widened. "What the—?"

Nikolai scowled.

The bodies of the hellbeasts had burst into silent flames that rapidly withered to wisps of fiery ash. Soon, all that remained of their presence was a dark stain on the carpet and the fading smell of sulfur.

CHAPTER FIVE

ABRAHAM WHITWORTH STARED. "THEY JUST VANISHED?"

"Yeah." Mae made a face. "It kinda resembled what happened to the devils I used *Decimate* on, in that crypt in Prague where the Dark Council had laid a trap for us. But they didn't erupt into flames like these ones did."

Bryony's aide looked dubious at her words.

"The only time demons and hellbeasts' bodies break down in a similar manner is when a holy blade kills them," Alicia Calvarro said with a frown.

The Queen of Soul Reapers turned FBI special agent touched the scythe pendant at the base of her throat distractedly.

She is correct, my witch, Brimstone said. *I recall Azazel saying something similar.*

I do too, Hellreaver concurred.

They were in Bryony's office, at the New York coven's headquarters. Though the hour was late, Alicia had responded to their call to attend the impromptu meeting when she'd found out about the hellbeasts. Astarte, the goddess turned demon general who headed the alliance of fallen angels determined to stop Satanael from destroying the world at the End of Days, had tasked her with keeping watch on the Sorcerer King and Barquiel's activities involving the Underworld.

Mae pondered Alicia's words with a faint frown. "So, when you say a holy blade, you mean like the guy in Chicago?"

The Soul Reaper queen dipped her head.

Bryony straightened. "That's right. Violet and Miles would know."

"Where are they, by the way?" Mae said curiously. "I haven't seen them in several days."

"They're attending a family reunion. One of their cousins got engaged."

Nikolai studied Alicia with a troubled expression. "So, if it wasn't a holy blade that did that to them, what did?"

Alicia was quiet for a moment. "The only other thing I can think of is that it was some kind of delayed destruction spell."

Mae's scalp prickled at her words. "A delayed destruction spell?"

Brimstone's ears twitched, his expression alert.

Alicia met their wary gazes, her unease plain to see. "Like a time bomb."

Mae's mind raced in the tense hush that followed. The more it seemed that tonight's incident might have been a fluke, the more her instincts screamed at her that it was anything but.

I believe you are right, my witch, Brimstone said with a low growl. *This is too much of a coincidence to be called mere chance.*

Something dawned on her then.

"A bomb needs a trigger." She looked at Nikolai, her stomach churning with an unnamed dread. "I wonder if we were the trigger."

His eyes darkened. "I never heard of a spell like that when I was working for the Dark Council."

Alastair ruffled his wings uneasily on the sorcerer's shoulder.

"Could it have been someone else?" Abraham suggested. "Or just a weird twist of fate?"

Alicia's frown deepened. "Portals to Hell don't just open randomly. I doubt one suddenly appearing under Mae's apartment was an accident."

"I concur," Bryony said grimly. "This has to be the work of the Dark Council."

Barquiel's face and that of his Immortal scientist protégé Dietrich Farago rose in Mae's mind. She clenched her jaw.

Ten bucks says they've got something to do with this.

Brimstone's hackles rose at that.

"Have there been any unusual incidents of late in the magic community?" Mae asked Bryony and Abraham. "Anything that might suggest what the Dark Council could be up to?"

Bryony shook her head, dashing her hopes for a clue. "No. The only thing that happened this week was the Boston coven approaching us for our assistance on a certain matter."

"The Boston coven?"

Bryony made a face. "They think they've got a haunted church on their hands. Several of their witches and sorcerers got sick when they went to investigate the place after reports of strange noises and lights."

"Ghosts in the sense humans understand them don't exist," Alicia said. "I should know." She paused. "But the remains of the dead are something else."

Mae digested this for a moment.

"Sick how?" she asked Bryony warily.

"Headaches and nausea. They want one of us to check it out." Bryony cast a shrewd look at Nikolai. "I was going to ask you to go, actually. Their High Priestess thought a white magic user would be of benefit."

"Your care for my health and safety warms the cockles of my heart," Nikolai said drily.

Bryony waved a vague hand, undeterred. "I'm sure they just ate something bad."

"I'll come with you," Mae said firmly. "It's safer for us to be together if we're both being targeted," she added at his hesitant expression.

Nikolai faltered before bobbing his head.

Hellreaver stirred against her chest. *Does that mean you finally intend to mate with the—mmph, mmph!*

All eyes locked on the pendant Mae had just muzzled with her hand.

"What'd he say this time?" Abraham asked suspiciously.

"Nothing you need to know," she replied darkly.

Can't...breathe! Hellreaver wheezed.

They left the coven headquarters and returned to Ridgewood. Crime scene tape still blocked off the entrance to the cinema. Jared had gone to interview the college students Mae had saved. Though the ambulances that had attended the incident had long left, a thin crowd still hung around despite the heavy rain.

It wasn't every day something this strange happened in Ridgewood.

Mae and Nikolai chatted briefly to the detective Jared had left in charge before taking the stairs to the apartment. The official story was that a group of oversized feral dogs had burst into the movie house and attacked the people inside. They'd disappeared just as quickly after Mae and Nikolai had scared them away. Animal control was supposedly on the lookout for them.

Mae grimaced as she and Nikolai entered her apartment. "I sure as hell hope animal control isn't really out there searching for missing hellbeasts."

"They'll be looking for a long time." Nikolai kicked off his wet boots and headed for the bathroom. "I'm gonna take a hot shower and hit the sack."

He reached for his T-shirt and peeled it off.

Mae's mouth went dry as she stared at his broad shoulders and muscular back. Her gaze lingered on the scar Oscar Beneventi had inflicted on the sorcerer during the Trial of Blood.

"Same." She bit her lip. "Er, don't you need to grab pajamas or something?"

Nikolai turned, leaned an arm up against the

doorjamb, and arched an eyebrow. "Whatever for?"

Mae gulped at his teasing expression. *Oh Lord. Don't tell me he sleeps in the nude.*

The thought of the sorcerer lying naked in bed mere feet away from her own room started doing strange things to her pulse.

Calm down, my witch, Brimstone warned at her glassy expression. *It's just the adrenaline talking.*

She's drooling, Hellreaver remarked.

Alastair made a worried noise where he perched on the hallway console.

Nikolai's lips twitched, like he'd guessed the dirty direction her imagination had just taken. His hot gaze stayed on Mae as he slowly closed the door.

The sound of the shower coming on stirred her from her lust-induced daze.

Mae clenched her fists, her face hot. "Shit. That was close."

Tell me about it, Brimstone groaned. *I seriously thought you were gonna attack him for a second there. Maybe we should buy a replacement for Bob.*

Mae's thoughts strayed to her trusty and defunct vibrator. It had met an untimely demise a while back, courtesy of a curious demon fox.

"How do you know about Bob?" she muttered as they headed for her bedroom.

Brimstone grunted. *Ryu enlightened me.*

Mae grimaced. Considering her sister was currently sleeping with Noah Tegner, the sorcerer assigned to the Jins' protection, she had zero need for sex toys. Especially since it seemed Noah was a total beast in the sack.

"Appearances sure are deceptive," she said glumly.

I know, Brimstone concurred. *You look like butter wouldn't melt in your mouth most days.*

Mae scowled, dumped Hellreaver on the bed, and stormed inside the bathroom.

She spared a thought for her landlord as she stepped under the shower. Mr. Seong was a frail octogenarian who also owned the movie theater. The last thing he needed was for the place to become the scene of a major crime.

At least no one died.

She'd assured him she would help look after things when she'd called him that evening to tell him what had happened. Luckily, the guy Mr. Seong had hired to manage the place was not prone to fits of hysteria.

She grimaced as she dried herself and wrapped a towel around her body. *I bet this is already all over Mrs. Son-Ha's network.*

Myung Ki Son-Ha was Koreatown's number one matriarch and chief gossip. She was better than the CIA at information gathering, so much so Mae wondered whether she'd been a spy in a previous life.

She stepped out of the bathroom and rocked to a halt.

Brimstone and Hellreaver were rooting around in her lingerie drawer. They froze when they sensed her horrified stare.

"What the heck are you doing?" Mae squeaked.

We decided not to stand in the way of what your loins want, my witch, Brimstone confessed sheepishly.

Hellreaver came out with one of Vlad's risqué gifts draped delicately over a blade. *Why don't you put this on and mosey on down the corridor to claim the sorcerer?*

Mae crossed the floor in three quick strides, snatched the lace and silk contraption, picked up Brimstone by his scruff and Hellreaver by his knuckleduster, and dumped them both in the corridor.

"You two are sleeping outside tonight!" she hissed before slamming the door shut.

Brimstone's faint whine came through the wood. *Oh come on! Where's your sense of humor?*

He scratched at the door.

I think her libido ate it, Hellreaver stated.

CHAPTER SIX

THE HIGH PRIESTESS OF THE CARACAS COVEN DIPPED IN a deferential bow.

"I am pleased to make your acquaintance, Witch Queen," she murmured gravely.

"Please, call me Mae," Mae said hastily.

Surprise darted across Valentina Flores's face. The older witch straightened, her expression relaxing into a faint smile. "It seems the rumors I heard about you are true. You don't like to stand on ceremony."

"It kinda makes me uncomfortable," Mae confessed.

Nikolai noted Bryony's chagrined face and hid a smile behind his champagne glass. Mae refusing to stand on ceremony was a constant source of exasperation for her.

He became aware of the Caracas High Priestess's guarded stare. Considering his affiliation with the Dark Council a mere three months ago, he was hardly surprised at the somewhat cool reception he had received at the parties Bryony had cornered him and Mae into attending.

"It is good to finally meet you, Mr. Stanisic," Valentina said in a neutral tone.

Nikolai dipped his chin curtly. "Nikolai is fine."

The High Priestess and her party chatted to them briefly before taking their leave. Mae sagged after they left.

"What's gotten into you?" Bryony asked sharply.

Penley meowed softly where she cradled him in her arms.

"Nothing," Mae replied sullenly.

Nikolai had an inkling about the reason for Mae's foul mood. His guarded gaze swept the elegant hall.

Chateau Monteville, the venue Abraham had chosen to host the reception the New York coven was holding in honor of their visiting South American brethren, was an opulent five-star hotel with views over Central Park. The Élysée Room was a stunning ballroom modeled after neoclassical architecture and had enough iconic marble columns and crystal chandeliers to sink a luxury ship.

Nikolai would have appreciated the decor even more were it not for the fact that he and Mae were the focus of everyone's attention where they stood in the garden court. A limestone fountain babbled pleasantly in the center of the atrium, the jets of water spouting off it reflecting light off the stained-glass roof and across the lush greenery filling the space.

They'd only been there half an hour and had already greeted twenty people. It seemed practically every major South American coven had sent representatives to New York to meet them.

"We're like hostages on a glitzy stage," Mae said sourly.

"Tell me about it," Nikolai murmured in agreement.

"Honestly, it's about time you two got used to these functions," Bryony said, unrepentant.

Nikolai glimpsed the bold gazes some of the witches were directing at him. He ran a finger discreetly around the collar of his suit. "Now I know what a prized stud feels like."

Alastair made a comforting sound on his shoulder.

Bryony waved away his fears. "Pish posh. Everyone knows you're a potential consort for Mae. No one would dare approach you with that intention in mind."

Mae's mouth flattened into a thin line. "That's not what their eyes are saying."

Pleasure quickened Nikolai's pulse. *Is she jealous?*

Mae's stomach growled.

He wilted a little. *No, I was right on the money the first time.*

Lines furrowed Bryony's brow. "Don't tell me the reason you're being so irritable is because you're hungry?"

Mae scowled. "You bet I am, lady. Why is party food so—" she waved a hand, "sparse? You'd think with the price tag this place fetched to host this event, they'd serve at least a roasted hog or three."

Nikolai couldn't help smiling then. Even though being here had not been high on either of their agendas of fun things to do on a Friday night, he was glad they'd come out. It had been two days since the attack in Ridgewood. The New York coven was no further along with their investigation into why a random group of hellbeasts had appeared under Mae's apartment. As for Alicia, her trip to the Underworld hadn't revealed fresh clues either. He was aware Mae was growing increasingly frustrated that they hadn't figured out what the Dark Council's goals were yet.

His smile faded. *To be fair, so I am.*

Not knowing what their enemy could be up to made it that much harder to defend themselves.

"This isn't a medieval soirée," Abraham chided. "You'll have to do with canapés."

Mae sneered. "Canapés are for sissies."

Brimstone licked his chops. Hellreaver quivered on her chest.

Hope brightened Mae's eyes as she listened to the familiar and the weapon. "There's a new all-you-can-eat Chinese buffet three streets down from here?"

"Don't even think about it," Abraham warned.

A waiter came up to them with a tray of finger food and a polite smile pasted across his face. "Would you like some—?"

Mae took the tray from him before he finished his sentence. "Don't mind if I do." She wolfed down two of the entrées, chewed twice, and swallowed. "What is this?"

The man's smile faded like mist on a sunny day. "Hmm, smoked salmon and caviar. Can I have my tray back please?"

"Leave it," Abraham said in a surly voice. "And bring

us another couple of those trays. She'll burn the place down if we don't get more food in her."

"Hey!" Mae protested.

The waiter rushed off with a worried expression.

Brimstone leaned heavily against Mae's leg. She grimaced at her familiar and her bristling weapon. "You sure you want some? It's raw fish eggs."

Brimstone made retching noises. Hellreaver stopped quivering.

A familiar aura washed over Nikolai. He stiffened at the sight of the man who appeared through the parting crowd like the proverbial Messiah.

"Why is he here?" he ground out.

"I invited him," Bryony said briskly.

Vlad ignored Nikolai's barely suppressed glower, his white Bengal tiger Tarang padding silently at his side. The familiar's tail started swinging vigorously when he spotted Brimstone.

The incubus kissed Bryony's cheek while Tarang and the fox shared friendly head bumps. He turned to Mae, gave her a dazzling smile that made several witches and sorcerers flush, and took her hand.

"And how's my future wife doing this evening?" Vlad drawled, his eyes glinting with a banked heat.

Color stained Mae's cheekbones. Vlad leaned down and pressed a kiss to her knuckles.

Nikolai's fist tightened around the stem of his flute.

Abraham took another drink off a passing waiter and downed it with the look of a man who knew his evening was about to go from tiresome to migraine-inducing.

Vlad flashed Nikolai a mocking look before inspecting Mae's knee-length, green sequin dress and matching high heels with a stare that lingered far too long for his liking.

"They suit you well, princess." He touched her left earlobe lightly. "You should have worn the emerald earrings I gave you."

Mae gulped. Abraham cast a worried glance at Nikolai.

Bryony leaned sideways toward Mae.

"He gave you emerald earrings?!" she hissed out of the corner of her mouth.

Mae nodded mutely. She bit her lip, her ears reddening.

Hellfire Magic flooded Nikolai's veins before he could stop himself. His champagne started steaming. Abraham groaned.

Vlad's pupils flared with redness as he narrowed his eyes at Nikolai.

"Seriously, you guys need to tone that shit down," someone grunted behind them.

Nikolai turned.

Enrique Cortes was strolling toward them at the head of a party of sorcerers and witches, his dark tuxedo and slicked-back hair adding to his usual aura of menace. A red Macaw with intelligent, golden eyes and a smart, black bow tie was perched his shoulder.

CHAPTER SEVEN

Mae relaxed, relieved at the distraction. At the rate things were going between Nikolai and Vlad, she was worried the hotel would get destroyed before the reception ended.

"It's good to see you again." She eyed the Colombian's outfit with a smile. "You scrub up nice."

"Yeah, well, I have to wear a lot of monkey suits in my line of work," Cortes muttered. "And black works best for blood."

Several members of his party blanched.

Mae rolled her eyes. "Murder jokes, really?"

Cortes's lips twitched. Surprise darted across his face when Mae pressed a peck to his cheek. The move drew the stares of every witch and sorcerer around them. A wave of murmurs broke out across the ballroom.

Abraham pinched the bridge of his nose. A lazy smile curved Vlad's mouth. Nikolai sighed.

"What was that for?" Cortes asked Mae warily.

"You did that deliberately, didn't you?" Bryony grumbled.

Mae put on an innocent air. "I don't know what you mean."

Bryony met Cortes's confused gaze. "Congratulations. The Witch Queen just acknowledged you as the future High Priest of the Medellin coven."

Cortes blinked. "Oh."

His entourage fidgeted awkwardly where they hovered behind him. It was clear many didn't appreciate this turn of events. Cortes cast a frown at them over his shoulder. They froze and lowered their gazes.

"What'd you do to them?" Vlad asked drily.

"Nothing I can repeat in polite company." Cortes focused on Mae. "I have the High Priest position covered. You don't need to go out of your way to help me."

Mae patted his arm and smiled. "It won't hurt. Besides, we're friends, aren't we?"

Cortes squinted. "You know I'm not interested in becoming one of your consorts, right?"

Mae's smile faded into a grimace. "Like I need another one of those headaches in my life." She caught Nikolai and Vlad's pointed stares, cleared her throat guiltily, and turned to the parrot bobbing excitedly on the Columbian's shoulder. "I like the bow tie, Popo."

"Hello, queen of my heart and future mistress!" Cortes's familiar gushed effusively. He flapped his wings. "I must say, you look like a dazzling rose among all these weeds tonight. Let me give you a hug, you buxom temptress!"

Mae winced as Cortes caught the parrot mid-flight.

Nikolai sneered. "Buxom temptress?"

"I swear, his vocabulary gets worse every time we meet him," Vlad told Cortes.

Popo became the object of narrow-eyed stares from the closest weeds around them while he struggled in his sorcerer's grip.

Cortes's lips thinned as his familiar's feathers smacked his face repeatedly. "What did I say to you before we left the hotel?"

Popo stiffened at his deadly tone. He went still, feathers drooping. "You said I was to behave."

"And how did I tell you to behave?"

The parrot's voice grew sullen. "You told me to keep my beak shut."

Hellreaver sniggered.

Mae frowned at the weapon. "Don't laugh. You're just as bad as him." She studied Cortes curiously while he returned a chastised Popo to his shoulder. "I wanted to ask. Won't becoming High Priest affect your standing in the cartel?"

Cortes's face grew inscrutable. "My boss and I have…come to an agreement. He's granted me a one-year sabbatical to settle my status in the magic community. I'll continue to assist him on the side when the need arises."

Vlad arched an eyebrow. "That's mighty nice of him."

Mae's belly tightened as she digested the

Colombian's words. She turned to Vlad. "Does this mean you would have to give up your seat in the *Black Devils* if you became my consort?"

Vlad shrugged dismissively at her brittle words. "I'll deal with that problem if it arises."

A commotion drew their attention before Mae could probe him further. A large delegation had just entered the Élysée Room. The witches and sorcerers belonging to it bumped the other guests rudely aside as they made a bee line for the atrium. From the scowls their rough behavior earned, the other covens recognized them.

A rotund man with bronze skin, a greasy expression, and enough gold adorning his figure to bankroll a new business strode briskly at their head, an imposing harpy eagle on his shoulder.

Nikolai straightened. Vlad narrowed his eyes.

Alastair and Popo stilled, their wary gazes locking on the eagle. Even Brimstone and Tarang grew alert.

"That's Sergio Mendes, the High Priest of the Rio de Janeiro coven." Bryony directed a warning look at Nikolai and Vlad. "Be nice. We need him on our side."

Vlad's brow furrowed. "Why?"

"Because he's rich," the witch replied tartly.

"Funny." Cortes's tone had grown cold. "No one told me the Rio de Janeiro High Priest was this strong."

Bryony looked discomfited. "I didn't think you'd care. Besides, it's not like you and I talk all the time."

"That'll change once I become High Priest," Cortes said confidently.

Mae glanced at the Columbian. "You can see his magic core?"

"No. But I can sense his power."

It wasn't just Mendes and his familiar's cores that told Mae they were strong. She could see a faint aura fluttering around the sorcerer and the eagle. Recognition flared.

"Enrique, does that guy have—?" she started awkwardly.

"Yes. He's an Arcane Magic user. And it seems he's showing off his powers to try and intimidate us." Cortes's expression turned flinty. "That asshole might as well be walking down the street with his fly open."

"How about you dial down the murder vibe?" Mae pursed her lips. "Seriously, you have scary eyes right now."

Cortes grunted.

Mendes and his entourage crowded around them seconds later. Mae frowned. It was clear the move was intended to keep the other covens at bay.

Mendes greeted Bryony, ignored everyone else, and fixed Mae with an intense stare that make Nikolai and Vlad's fingers curl into fists.

Uh-oh, Brimstone murmured. *Your future spouses look like they're on the war path.*

Mendes took her hand with sweaty fingers and planted a kiss on her knuckles. "We finally meet, my queen."

CHAPTER EIGHT

"Ugh," Mae croaked.

Mendes slowly released her hand, confused. "Pardon?"

Mae noted Bryony's leaden stare.

"It's, er, nice to make your acquaintance," she told Mendes with a glassy smile.

A *sotto voce* conversation distracted her as the man started fawning over her.

"How about I pin him down and you hit him?" Vlad murmured coldly to Nikolai.

"We should give Abraham our jackets to hold," the sorcerer contributed in a savage tone. "They charge more for dry cleaning blood out of these suits."

"I am NOT holding your jackets!" Abraham hissed.

"I'll hold them," Cortes volunteered icily.

Mae spotted the death stare Bryony cast at the four men out of the corner of her eye.

Crimson flared in Brimstone's pupils as he glared at Mendes. *Should I bite his arm off?!*

A sorcerer in Mendes's entourage overheard the whispered exchange between Vlad and Nikolai. He bristled and unleashed the sword hidden within the bracelet on his arm, his ferret baring its teeth where it coiled around his neck.

"How insolent!"

A threatening growl rumbled from Tarang.

Mendes's eagle cracked her wings open and landed in front of the tiger with a shrill cry. Tarang blinked, surprised. He recovered and bared his fangs at her.

Golden magic detonated around the bird. Mae's skin prickled. Even Mendes looked startled at his familiar's reaction. Vlad took a step toward the harpy bobbing her head threateningly at Tarang.

Mae touched his arm. "It's okay."

A surprised sound escaped the eagle in the next instant.

Brimstone had stepped out from behind Tarang.

The crimson aura around the fox deepened, the feral growl vibrating from his chest making the familiars in the vicinity who were not his friends whimper and hide behind their sorcerers and witches. His magic warmed Mae's blood and sent Hellreaver trembling against her chest.

Brimstone snarled.

The harpy fell to the floor under the sheer force of his demonic influence. An angry squawk left her. Her feathers trembled as she tried to fight his dominance.

"I—I apologize profusely, my queen!" Mendes mumbled. "I don't know what's come over her."

Sweat beaded his brow as he picked up the eagle

and cradled her to his chest, his face ashen. He winced when she scratched him with her claws. The harpy glowered at Brimstone.

Mae stared. *Does he not have control over her?*

Brimstone cocked his head, equally puzzled. *It seems not.*

The hairs rose on Mae's nape before she could make sense of the fear she'd just glimpsed in Mendes's eyes. Brimstone straightened, ears pricking to and fro. Hellreaver growled and transformed before coming to a defensive hover in front of her.

Nikolai tensed.

Vlad glanced at her, his expression alert. "Mae?"

The sorcerer and the incubus drew sharp breaths when they finally perceived the vile pressure thickening the air in the ballroom. Agitated murmurs broke out amongst the witches and sorcerers attending the reception as they too detected the change in the atmosphere.

"What is that?" Cortes asked, his wary gaze sweeping the hall for an enemy they could not yet see.

Mae clenched her jaw. "It's the power of Hell."

Bryony and Abraham exchanged a worried glance.

White magic flared on Nikolai's fingertips and in Alastair's eyes. The sorcerer's watch shifted into a spear.

A crimson aura distorted the air around Vlad. "Is it Barquiel?"

The diamond studs in his ears dropped into his hands and morphed into dark swords brimming with demonic light.

"I don't know. But it's a portal for sure." Mae's pulse raced as she scanned the ballroom and the atrium, trying to gauge where it might open. "We should get everyone out of here," she told Bryony grimly.

The witch nodded stiffly and headed for the center of the noisy ballroom with Abraham.

"Ladies and gentlemen, it seems we have an emergency," Bryony said calmly above the restless brouhaha. "We would be grateful if you could leave the reception hall in an orderly fashion."

The Chateau Monteville's event manager approached her and Abraham with a confused frown. His staff similarly exchanged puzzled glances where they still circulated around the hall.

Movement had Mae's gaze jerking to the right. Shadows were pooling at the east end of the ballroom. Valentina Flores and her coven unleashed their magic as they observed the corrupt phenomenon with narrowed eyes. Cold fingers danced down Mae's spine as the acrid smell of sulfur coiled around the hall.

Too late!

Brimstone swelled into his nine-tailed demonic spirit form, his giant head knocking aside the branches of palm trees and chandeliers. Shocked cries sounded from the covens who had yet to witness his true appearance.

I smell a lot of hellbeasts, Hellreaver warned.

I do too, the fox rumbled.

His vibrating tails made the air hum, the crimson aura dancing on his fur pulsing through the bond that linked them.

Twin spheres of Moon Magic and white magic exploded above Nikolai's fingers. He looked over at Mae, a muscle jumping in his cheek. "This is probably what happened under your apartment."

Vlad glanced between them with narrowed eyes.

"What happened under her apartment?" he asked the sorcerer.

"A group of hellbeasts turned up at the movie theater and attacked civilians. They weren't much of a challenge."

Vlad leveled an accusing scowl at him. "How come you didn't tell me about this?!"

"Because we don't know what we're dealing with yet," Nikolai replied briskly. "Besides, I don't recall owing you anything."

"Now's really not the time for you guys to be having a lovers' spat," Cortes snapped.

Popo leaned forward on his shoulder, Arcane Magic brightening his pupils as he gripped his sorcerer's flesh with his claws.

Mae followed their unblinking stares. Her stomach lurched.

Darkness was coalescing at the west end of the ballroom.

Vlad's knuckles whitened on his blades. "Is that a second portal?"

My witch! Brimstone warned.

The fox was looking at the ceiling. Mae's head snapped up. Her eyes widened.

The glass roof was rippling.

"Shit!"

Heat swelled in her veins as she called upon her magic.

The roof of the atrium exploded just as she unleashed *Devour*.

CHAPTER NINE

A SHIELD MADE OF MOON MAGIC EXPLODED BENEATH Mae's spell as it swallowed the deadly glass fragments and hellbeasts raining down upon them from the third portal that had appeared overhead.

Screams erupted across the garden court when the monsters who'd avoided *Devour* landed on Nikolai's barrier with heavy thuds. More came from the ballroom, where the other portals had opened.

Vlad observed the creatures attempting to rip Nikolai's shield to shreds with a heavy scowl. "Those are hellbeasts?"

Tarang's hackles rose beside him.

"Yes," Mae said in a hard voice.

Relief shot through her as she scanned the ballroom.

Despite looking shocked at the sight of the monsters, the sorcerers and witches of the South American covens had successfully erected defenses against the beasts pacing the floor threateningly around them. For once, Mae was grateful for the presence of so many High Priests and Priestesses under one roof.

Valentina assisted Bryony and Abraham where they protected the Chateau Monteville employees cowering at the far end of the hall, their barriers shimmering brightly. Though they could not see the magic nor the scores of familiars hidden from their view in the ballroom, there was no way the hotel staff could miss the nightmarish creatures that had emerged from the portals and who were now watching them with hateful eyes.

"Jared is gonna be so pissed," Mae mumbled under her breath.

A flash of gold drew her eyes. Cortes was holding a whip and an antique sword brimming with Arcane Magic in his hands.

She stared. "Those are new."

"They're family heirlooms." The Columbian met her slightly suspicious squint with a blasé shrug. "I borrowed them."

Mae directed a questioning look at Popo.

"He totally stole them," the familiar blurted out shamelessly. The bird's wings blazed gold as he augmented his sorcerer's magic. "Ready to kick some ass, Enrique?!"

Cortes's expression grew pinched. "I'll have less of that trash talk from you, thank you very much."

As if responding to some silent signal, the beasts on the ground finally attacked. Cortes's whip cracked the air as a hellboar charged at him. The beast shrieked when the lashes wrapped around its neck.

The sorcerer widened his stance, yanked on the weapon, and sent the monster crashing into a limestone urn. Pale shards filled the air. The hellboar tried to get back on its feet. Its screech of rage turned into a choked gurgle as Cortes slit its throat with his sword.

Crimson light engulfed Vlad and Tarang as they faced off against two hellwolves. The tiger lunged at breakneck speed and sank his fangs into the closest monster's jugular. Vlad blocked the second wolf as it prepared to pounce on his familiar, the demonic energy that blasted from his body on a roar sending the creature smashing sideways into a tree.

Mae blinked. *He's gotten stronger!*

"Brim, stay here and help Bryony and Abraham get everyone to safety!" She studied the beasts clawing at Nikolai's pale barrier with narrowed eyes before meeting the sorcerer's tense gaze. "On the count of three?!"

Nikolai nodded. "One. Two. *Three!*"

He retracted his shield.

"*Wind Fury!*" Mae barked.

Her magic detonated across the atrium on a dark red wave that shoved Nikolai, Vlad, and Cortes back a couple of feet and sent others tumbling to the ground with surprised cries. Deadly currents wrapped around the hellbeasts dropping toward the garden court. The monsters screeched, momentum halted as they found themselves frozen in midair by the violent, magical whirlwinds.

Mae levitated in their midst, her hair and dress fluttering faintly in a storm of her own creation. Claws clanged against Hellreaver's blades as he flashed around her and deflected the creatures' attempts to maim her.

Power throbbed through Mae and resonated across the bond connecting her to the weapon and Brimstone. She lifted a hand to the sky and called forth another spell.

"Eclipse!"

The dark void that bloomed silently above the gaping roof of the atrium obscured the stars in the sky and distorted the air with a flood of negative pressure. The trees in the garden court trembled violently as they bowed and were nearly uprooted. The jets spouting from the fountains rose against gravity.

The shrieks of the captive hellbeasts made Mae's ears ring as they were swallowed by *Eclipse*. Blood pounded dully in her skull when she ended the spell a moment later.

Corruption washed across her flesh before she could draw her next breath.

Two more portals had opened in the garden court. Her eyes rounded. Scores of monsters poured out of them and bounded toward the reception hall.

Mae cursed and dove, Hellreaver at her side.

Nikolai's wrathful shout halted them in their tracks. *"MOON FIRE!"*

A wall of pale flames burst into life before the

sorcerer's outstretched fingers. It raced across the atrium and swept through the ballroom in the blink of an eye.

Goosebumps prickled Mae's flesh as Nikolai's magic wrapped around half the beasts and sent them screaming fitfully while it consumed their flesh in an unholy blaze.

He's gotten stronger too!

Hellfire and Moon Magic licked at Nikolai's skin and danced on Alastair's wings as they focused on destroying the new horde. Vlad and Cortes turned their attention to eliminating the hellbeasts in the atrium. Mae was about to go help them when heat pulsed through her belly, startling her. Her gaze found Brimstone.

The demonic fox's tails quivered violently where he framed the exit with his body, the sheer force emanating from him pushing back the swarm of monsters trying to attack him and the people escaping the ballroom. Bryony and Abraham grunted on his left as a pair of hellhounds smashed into their shields. Valentina cursed on the fox's right. She and a High Priest were pushed back by the beasts trying to get past their barriers.

A hellwolf raked Brimstone's foot with its claws. The fox lowered his muzzle to snap at the beast. The quills of a hellboar pierced his face and narrowly missed his eyes. Brimstone winced before baring his fangs, pupils flaring crimson.

Fury twisted Mae's belly as she arrowed across the ballroom.

Hellreaver shot past her in a red blur. He let out a sound that made several beasts fall to the ground in terror and sliced off the heads of the monsters that had hurt the fox. The dead hellwolf's head spun comically through the air before landing with a wet sound in front of a sorcerer crawling along the floor.

Scarlet drops splashed onto Sergio Mendes's ashen face and clothes. A horrified croak escaped him. He backpedaled across the ground and tripped a cursing witch and sorcerer.

Mae narrowed her eyes. *Why isn't he using his magic?!*

Mendes met her gaze. Fear widened his pupils. He looked around wildly, as if searching for something.

There was movement at the corner of Mae's vision. Heat bloomed on her arm before she could react. She startled.

The harpy eagle squawked loudly as she rose and vanished through the gaping roof of the atrium. Mae looked from the disappearing bird to the fresh scratch on her skin, confused.

What the hell?!

An angry sound from Brimstone distracted her. Four hellhounds had latched onto his flank and were trying their best to tear open his flesh.

She gritted her teeth. *"Hellreaver!"*

The weapon returned to her hand with a loud clap. Mae raised him to the sky and drew on their combined strength. Fire bubbled through her veins as the power of three surged inside her.

"DECIMATE!"

A black and crimson orb detonated into existence around Hellreaver. The light flickered violently. Tremors shook the foundation of the building.

Dark lightning streaked with vermilion threads crackled ominously within the sphere and danced wildly on the weapon's blades. Mae felt Hellreaver swell in her grip a second before he released a veritable storm of deadly electrical arcs.

The currents zapped across the ballroom with explosive thumps that made Mae's ears throb and caused the very air to vibrate. They pierced the hellbeasts attacking Brimstone and arrowed toward the remaining creatures in the hall, their movements defying physics as they multiplied.

The monsters were wiped out in a matter of seconds.

Deafening silence fell when the last one vanished in a cloud of black ash. The stench of sulfur started to fade as the remains of the hellbeasts settled in a thick layer of soot.

Mae ended *Decimate,* her chest heaving with her breaths.

The magnitude of the spell she had just unleashed had drained her.

Hellreaver wriggled out of her hand and shot into her arms. *My witch!*

Mae landed on the ground and hugged him, relief tightening her chest. The floor trembled as Brimstone approached. He lowered his head and pressed his brow against Mae's, his magic warming her flesh even as his wounds healed.

"*I'm glad you're both safe,*" the fox rumbled.

Hellreaver whined and nudged him with a blade. They shifted back into their smaller forms.

Mae stared past the awestruck faces of the witches and sorcerers watching her from across the ballroom and met Bryony's strained gaze. The older witch's expression and Abraham's fraught look told her they would not be able to sweep this incident under the carpet and keep it from the eyes and ears of the city's officials. Not with so many human witnesses around.

"Jared is gonna go bananas," she mumbled.

Brimstone huffed.

Someone called her name. She turned.

Nikolai and Vlad were hurrying across the floor toward her, Cortes trailing in their steps. The tension humming through Mae drained out of her, rendering her weak.

Though the sorcerer and the incubus looked annoyed enough to tear someone's head off, they were both uninjured.

Vlad clasped her shoulders tightly and raked her figure with a worried stare. "Are you alright?!"

"I'm fine."

Tarang and Brimstone brushed against each other with comforting rumbles.

Nikolai scowled at Vlad. "How about you let go of her, asshole? You look like you're gonna break her bones."

The incubus loosened his hold on Mae guiltily. He glared at the sorcerer. "Back off, Moon Boy."

Mae swallowed a sigh.

Cortes arched an eyebrow. "Want me to take care of them for you?"

She grimaced. "Somehow, I get the feeling that sentence involves burying bodies."

Cortes's lips twitched. He stiffened when Popo started grooming his hair with his beak.

"Who's the bestest sorcerer in the world, huh?" the parrot crooned lovingly. "Come here, let me give you a hug!"

Cortes growled. "I swear to God, I will skin you alive if—"

His familiar's colorful wings struck him in the face and muffled the rest of his threat.

CHAPTER TEN

"YOU GUYS ARE GONNA GIVE ME AN ULCER," JARED grumbled.

"Yeah, well, this isn't exactly how I anticipated my Friday night going either," Mae muttered.

Jared eyed her dress before glancing toward the ballroom. "Was this one of those schmooze parties Bryony insists you guys attend? The ones you and Nikolai keep bitching about?"

Bryony's expression grew pinched. Mae avoided her accusatory stare.

They were standing in a hallway in Chateau Monteville. Lights from the ambulances and fire engines parked on the road outside washed across the interior of the Élysée Room through what remained of the roof of the atrium. Although there had been injuries among the guests, none had been too serious. Luckily, there had been healers among the attending covens.

As for the hotel staff, they were pretty much suffering from shock at the horrors they'd witnessed.

Alicia appeared at the end of the corridor. She joined them and handed a bottle of antacids to Jared. "Here."

He eyed it like it was poison. "Is this from Hell?"

The Soul Reaper Queen made a face. "It's from the drugstore around the corner."

She looked beyond the NYPD officers guarding the entrance to the ballroom to the forensics team examining what remained of the hellbeasts.

"I know this is a rhetorical question, but are they really going to find any clues inspecting those?" Bryony said skeptically.

"No." Alicia frowned. "That ash will be gone in a few hours."

Mae had to concur. The same thing had happened at the movie theater.

She chewed her lip and squinted at Jared. "How bad is this gonna be?"

"On a scale of one to ten? Twenty," the Immortal said sourly.

Mae slumped.

"The Special Affairs Bureau is already on my ass looking for answers as to why monsters from Hell are suddenly terrorizing this city," Jared added.

He directed a shrewd look at Alicia.

The Reaper Queen shrugged. "Hey, I'm as much in the dark as you are."

They leveled a questioning stare at Mae.

She sighed. "I still have no idea what this is about either."

Footsteps rose behind them. Mae turned.

Nikolai was headed their way with Valentina Flores.

"There are no signs of Sergio Mendes and his coven anywhere in the building," Nikolai reported in clipped tones. "Vlad and Cortes are out looking for clues to where they might have disappeared to." He lifted the carrier bags in his hands. "They got you guys these before they left."

Mae's stomach grumbled as the appetizing smell of burgers filled the air. Hellreaver started to drool.

Valentina looked on uneasily while Brimstone and the weapon wolfed down six burgers each in the blink of an eye.

"I still don't understand why Mendes and his coven didn't attack those creatures," Nikolai muttered.

It had become clear to everyone in the aftermath of the battle that the Rio de Janeiro sorcerers and witches had done nothing to aid their side.

The Caracas High Priestess furrowed her brow. "I must admit, he was like another man tonight. One I didn't recognize." The witch clocked Mae's surprised stare. "Don't get me wrong, Sergio is strong and he likes to show off his wealth, but his behavior and that of that harpy eagle were out of character." She paused, concern darkening her eyes. "In fact, I don't recall his familiar being a harpy eagle. I'm pretty sure it was a black hare."

Unease coiled through Mae. She chewed the mouthful of burger she'd just taken and swallowed.

What the hell is Vedran trying to do this time?

A low growl left Brimstone. *That I do not know, my witch.* The fox licked his chops. *But Barquiel is playing with fire. The Council of Hell will not look kindly upon him if he keeps bringing hellbeasts to Earth without their permission.*

Mae didn't realize she'd voiced her concerns out loud until Valentina addressed her.

"You believe this to be the work of the Sorcerer King?"

"There was a similar attack a few days ago, where Mae lives," Bryony explained at the Caracas High Priestess's guarded expression. "It was on a smaller scale than this one. But we still don't know what they're after."

"Well, if they were trying to rattle our cage, they've succeeded," Alicia said bitterly.

"Could Mendes be working for the Dark Council?" Mae asked Valentina.

Valentina hesitated. "I can't speak for the other South American covens, but I have never known Sergio or anyone in his entourage to show any inclination toward black magic."

Frustration churned Mae's stomach. She'd cast *Nullify* when the first portal had appeared. She was pretty confident there had been no black magic cores amidst the guests attending the reception or inside the hotel. Still, the more she relived what had taken place in the ballroom, the more certain she grew that Mendes had known about tonight's attack.

Though they were yet to see any evidence that the

Sorcerer King was behind these latest incidents, there was no doubt in her mind that it was the work of the Vedran and the demon archduke who worked for him. Whatever was happening was too intentional to be coincidence. And she could not get rid of the seed of suspicion that had taken root inside her tonight.

That she and Nikolai had been the intended targets.

Movement at the opposite end of the corridor distracted her from her dark thoughts. Abraham appeared from the direction of the main reception.

"I've managed to pacify the hotel manager for now," he told Bryony glumly. "The good news is this little stunt hasn't made the late-night headlines yet. The bad news is the mayor wants to see us tomorrow morning at eight thirty sharp."

Bryony groaned.

"Want me to come with you?" Mae volunteered.

Bryony and Abraham looked at her like she'd offered to parade naked in front of the mayor.

"You, the fox, and Hellreaver at City Hall?" Bryony grumbled. "Are you trying to give me a heart attack? Besides, all we need is for one of those damn portals to open there and we might as well kiss our coven headquarters goodbye."

Abraham pursed his lips, his gaze swinging between Mae and Nikolai. "Besides, aren't you two going to Marblehead tomorrow to look at that church?"

"What church?" Jared asked, nonplussed.

"The Boston coven asked Bryony for help investigating a haunted church," Nikolai explained with all the excitement of a man about to face death row.

Valentina raised an eyebrow. "There's no such thing as ghosts."

"That's what I said," Alicia muttered.

Valentina studied Jared and the FBI agent with a cautious stare.

She leaned toward Bryony. "I've been meaning to ask you for a while, but who are they?"

"That's Thod, the Queen of Soul Reapers." Bryony indicated Jared dismissively. "And he's an Immortal."

The detective narrowed his eyes.

Valentina had gone pale. "Oh. I heard rumors."

She hesitated, her wary gaze on Alicia.

"Yes?" Alicia said politely.

"Hmm." Valentina's expression brightened with an unhealthy degree of zeal. "Could I see the scythe?"

CHAPTER ELEVEN

A DARK MANTLE WAS OBSCURING THE HORIZON TO THE east by the time they reached the outskirts of Marblehead the next day.

"Looks like we're in for another storm," Mae murmured, her gaze on the distant sky.

Nikolai had to agree. The low-pressure system approaching the East Coast had given rise to a headache that made his temples throb.

A light rain started to fall as they exited Route 129 and headed onto Ocean Avenue. The end of the peninsula soon came into view, along with the isthmus connecting the island of Marblehead Neck to the mainland. New England-style properties dotted the rocky shoreline stretching out on either side of them. An imposing, red clock tower with a weathervane dominated the skyline beyond the fishing boats and leisure crafts bobbing in the harbor to the left. To the right, a seawall protected the road they were driving on from the foam-tipped waves racing across the turbulent surface of Massachusetts Bay.

Mae got a text from Abraham just as they reached the island. Her shoulders drooped. "The mayor is demanding the head of whoever was behind the attack at the hotel. Looks like that guy's not gonna let this go anytime soon."

"He's welcome to go to Budapest and have a talk with my father," Nikolai grunted.

"Your father would eat him for lunch." She sighed. "Let's get this over with and go home."

Nikolai's chest swelled a little at her words. Home. It was a word he'd never thought he would associate with himself again. Although life under his father's thumb had been wretched, his mother's presence had made things bearable and the suite they'd called their home in his castle had been as warm a place as she'd been allowed to make it amidst the austere conditions they'd lived under. All of that had ended the night she died. The rooms that had once been filled with her laughter had become a dismal prison that had trapped his soul in heavy chains he'd believed he would forever be burdened by.

He could never have imagined how much his life would change the night he made the fateful decision to break free from his father and his Dark Council. Despite the fact that he was only Mae's tenant, her apartment was the first place that had felt like somewhere he could call home again. One he hoped to share with her for a long time, if she chose him as her consort. Vlad's face flashed before him at that thought.

Of course, there's still that bastard to contend with.

He took a road that skirted the sea-facing coastline and soon pulled up at the address Bryony had given them.

Mae stared out the window. "You sure this is the place?"

Nikolai double checked the SUV's GPS and frowned. "Pretty sure."

He turned the wheel and guided the vehicle onto a road that was nothing more than a muddy track riddled with potholes. A low hill rose in the distance, beyond a depression in the rocky outcrop. On its brow, overlooking the ocean, sat an old, dilapidated church.

Brimstone climbed onto Mae's lap from the footwell and propped his paws on the dashboard, his ears and nose twitching curiously.

Nikolai glanced warily at the fox. "Is he sensing something?"

"Just the storm." Mae shivered. "I don't know about you, but that looks like the perfect setting for a horror movie."

He had to agree. The darkening sky was doing nothing to add to the ambiance. "I bet Cortes and Vlad would have a field day burying bodies here."

"Don't go putting ideas into their heads," Mae groaned. "I get enough questions about their day jobs as it is from my mom."

It had been midnight by the time Cortes and Vlad had caught up with them at the hotel last night, their vexation at not having uncovered where Mendes and his coven had vanished to clear. On the plus side, the gag order Jared and Alicia had imposed on the hotel staff who'd been in the ballroom seemed to have been effective. So far, news of what had transpired at the reception had not hit the morning headlines. As for the Dark Council, there had been no unusual movements reported by Nikolai's contacts when he'd checked in with them last night.

He frowned. Still, something was definitely up. He could feel it in his bones.

A car came into view when they cleared the dip. Nikolai parked behind it, grabbed his jacket from the backseat, and got out with Mae. Alastair settled on his shoulder in a soft rustle of feathers as he pulled up his hood.

Brimstone jumped out and landed in a puddle. Mud splashed his legs. He made an annoyed sound.

"Maybe we should get you a raincoat and boots," Mae suggested.

Brimstone sneered.

Mae grinned. "You'd look so cute. Like Little Red Riding Fox."

Hellreaver wheezed. Alastair gave the weapon a mildly disapproving look.

A woman stepped out of the car and came over to meet them.

"Are you from the New York coven?" she asked nervously.

Nikolai dipped his head. "We are."

The witch shook their hands. "I'm Leta Patton, from the Boston coven."

A sparrow poked its head out of her coat pocket.

The bird squeaked worriedly. Leta's gaze dropped to Brimstone. Her eyes widened in recognition.

She glanced at Alastair, shot a stunned look at Nikolai and Mae, and bowed hastily. "Forgive me! I didn't realize the Witch Queen and her consort were coming to investigate this matter personally."

Mae sighed. "There's no need to bow. Just…call me Mae. He's Nikolai."

Leta straightened, still uneasy despite her reassurance.

Nikolai indicated the abandoned church. "How long has this place been empty?"

Leta relaxed a little. "Some twenty odd years. The last pastor to serve here died around that time. The diocese never replaced him."

Mae tucked her hands in the pockets of her jacket. "Can you tell us what's been happening?"

"Sure. It started about a week ago. Some of the locals heard noises and saw strange lights coming from this place. At first, they assumed it was just kids fooling around. But then someone fell ill after they took their dog for a walk near the church. They thought it might have been a gas leak, but the gas engineers who came out to inspect the building didn't find anything untoward. It turns out the gas supply was cut off years ago." The witch's gaze shifted to the silent structure on the hill. "We were eventually called in when more people started becoming unwell."

"Bryony told us the sorcerers and witches who investigated the church complained of nausea and headaches?" Mae said curiously.

"Yes. I've only been here fifteen minutes and I'm starting to feel queasy as well," Leta mumbled, pale-faced. "The last time someone from our coven came to this place was three days ago."

Nikolai exchanged a neutral glance with Mae. He couldn't sense anything out of the ordinary, nor did he feel sick. Judging from Mae's expression, neither did she.

Could it be because of our magic?

"I'm afraid I have to leave," Leta said apologetically. "I have another appointment."

She chewed her lip, clearly torn at having to abandon them.

"It's okay," Nikolai said. "We'll be fine on our own."

Leta hesitated before nodding. They watched her leave.

"You got anything from *Nullify?*"

Mae's brow furrowed as she stared after the witch's disappearing car. "She's not a black magic user." She turned toward the church. "How about we take a look around?"

They climbed the stone steps leading to the building. An overgrown garden of tall grass and witch hazel had invaded the porch, the flowers' yellow petals the only points of brightness amidst the otherwise drab backdrop.

Nikolai had to give the door a good push with his shoulder to get it to shift. Wood creaked ominously when it finally swung open on rusty hinges.

CHAPTER TWELVE

A VESTIBULE STREWN WITH DEAD LEAVES AND DEBRIS came into view in the half-light. Beyond it was a nave lined with pews that had long since seen their best days.

Rain had formed puddles in a central aisle extending to a murky chancel. The only illumination came from pale, thin shafts arrowing through jagged holes where parts of the cradle vault had collapsed. The arched windows rising above the side aisles and in the shallow transepts had been boarded up for some time from the looks of the tarnished nails holding the planks together.

Lightning flashed outside as they ventured into the foyer. The bright afterglow scored shadows across Nikolai's retina. Thunder boomed almost immediately, the sound so loud it rattled the building.

"This place is seriously creeping me out," Mae mumbled.

Hellreaver quivered against her chest.

She squinted. "What do you mean, you want to go back to the car? You're a demonic weapon." Her mouth pressed into a thin line as she listened. "It's your own fault for staying up all night watching scary movies."

Hellreaver whined. Brimstone curled his lip in contempt.

Nikolai swallowed a sigh.

They decided to split up and headed into the side aisles.

Commemorative boards lined the wall under the windows Nikolai passed. The names scored into them had faded, the wood and the inscriptions damaged by exposure to the open elements. Broken votive candle holders glittered between the dirty cans and food wrappers underfoot as he proceeded up the gloomy corridor. He spotted a few bibles amidst the litter.

They explored the vestry and backrooms before meeting up in the chancel.

"Find anything?" Mae asked.

Nikolai frowned. "Nope."

She glanced around the church. "Maybe it was the local kids fooling around after all."

"That wouldn't explain the coven members' symptoms or those of the locals."

"Could the kids have been smoking some extremely potent pot?" Mae hazarded.

Nikolai grimaced. "I doubt that. Even if they had been, from the effects the coven reported, they'd be in a coma."

She sighed and tucked her hands inside the pockets

of her jacket. "You're right. It looks like this was a totally wasted trip. How about we grab an early dinner and head back?"

"We had lunch two hours ago."

Mae arched an eyebrow. "And your point is?"

Brimstone studied Nikolai with equal brazenness.

He rolled his eyes and headed into the central aisle. "At the rate at which you guys eat, we're gonna have to get second jobs to afford our food bills."

"Look, I can't help it, okay?" Mae protested, falling into step beside him. "I have a high metabolic rate. Granted, Brimstone and Hellreaver are just gluttons."

Brimstone stopped and growled.

Nikolai and Mae looked at him, surprised. The fox twisted around, his hackles rising. He stared at the chancel.

An uncanny sensation prickled Nikolai's nape as he followed the fox's gaze. Alastair grew still on his shoulder.

There was something in the church. Something he hadn't sensed until now. A faint undertone of darkness that danced at the very edges of his magic.

"Mae?"

"Yeah, I feel it too." Mae frowned, her expression focused. "Brim says there's a weird smell up ahead."

They joined the fox as he headed back into the chancel.

Mae stopped a few feet from the wooden altar rising beneath a boarded-up, stained-glass window, dropped on her haunches, and examined the cracked tiles Brimstone was sniffing at.

"Those look fresh."

Nikolai spotted the muddy footprints she'd seen amidst the decaying leaves. He squatted, touched one of the marks, and rubbed some of the dirt between his fingers before bringing it to his nose.

He frowned. "It's red clay."

Mae's face tightened. "I didn't see any red clay outside."

Unease churned Nikolai's stomach. "I'm pretty sure this island is made of volcanic rock."

They straightened, senses on alert.

"Didn't Leta say the last person from her coven was here a while ago?" Mae muttered.

"She did."

Another growl rumbled from Brimstone. Crimson shimmered around Hellreaver.

Alastair squawked threateningly and flapped his wings on his shoulder. Nikolai startled. Heat warmed his belly as he unleashed twin spheres of white and Moon Magic, the power thrumming through his veins making his muscles quiver.

Devour exploded above Mae's right hand.

"*Nullify!*" she barked.

Rain fell and thunder boomed in the fraught silence that ensued, echoing her voice. They scanned the interior of the church.

There was no one there.

The globes of magic flickered out above Nikolai's fingers. He lowered his hands, still on edge.

Mae narrowed her eyes. "Brim?"

The fox was glaring at something behind them.

A low susurration sounded in Nikolai's ears as he turned. His pulse quickened.

The altar was quivering.

Mae stared. "What the—?!"

The whispers grew louder. Ice crawled across Nikolai's scalp. He could hear a faint voice inside his head.

The altar came apart with a suddenness that made them gasp and drew a snarl from Brimstone. Nikolai's eyes rounded as the wooden pieces constituting the table levitated silently into the air.

His gut twisted when he saw what was hidden beneath it.

A square block made of obsidian rose from the foundations of the church. It was engraved with runes made of blue flames.

Darkness started pooling above it, the shadows inside the church converging onto the eerie monument as if it were drawing them in. They merged, forming a black globe that throbbed with corruption.

Mae's eyes glazed over. She took a step toward the stone block.

"Mae?!"

Alarm twisted Nikolai's stomach at the sight of her blank expression. He grabbed her arm.

She resisted his attempt to stop her.

Brimstone pawed at her leg with a soft whine. Hellreaver trembled against her chest.

Mae blinked and stopped. She shook her head, as if coming out of a daze. Awareness returned to her face.

She looked at Nikolai, confused. "What...just happened?"

Fear locked Nikolai's breath in his throat. A sinister energy was coiling through the church. The susurration intensified.

His heart thumped against his ribs as he drew on his white magic, the bond connecting him to Alastair flaring brightly inside him while he attempted to keep whatever was trying to get inside his mind out. "Mae! Use *Negate!*"

Mae nodded. Her lips parted. "*Ne...ga...*"

Her voice trailed off mid-incantation. Her expression became glassy. She took three steps toward the black stone and touched the roiling sphere atop it.

A silent wave boomed outward from the obsidian altar. It thumped in Nikolai's ears and lifted him off his feet. He caught a glimpse of Mae flying through the air as he sailed backward across the chancel. He crashed into the front pew of the nave. Pain lanced his flank.

Mae smashed through the opposite row with a grunt.

A cacophony of voices and images filled Nikolai's skull with his next heartbeat.

Alastair's panicked croaks reached him dimly as he fell to his knees. He clasped his head and tasted blood on his tongue as he bit down on his lip to stifle the scream bubbling up his throat. The vice-like pain squeezing his mind was like nothing he'd experienced before. He blinked, his vision hazy.

For a moment, he couldn't understand what he was seeing.

Debris was swirling through the church.

It was as if a storm had exploded inside the building.

The boards ripped from the windows with torturous sounds, exposing broken, cracked panes.

"*Shield!*" Mae barked.

Her barrier dropped around Nikolai a heartbeat before all the glass in the church imploded. The fragments bounced off Mae's defense as she climbed to her feet, the crimson aura engulfing her reflected around Brimstone and Hellreaver where they'd assumed their true forms at her side. She stumbled over to where Nikolai crouched.

"*Soul Shield!*" Mae growled. She resisted the tempest dragging at her limbs, dropped down on her knees, and wrapped her arms protectively around him. "*Multiply!*"

Brimstone crouched and curled his giant form around them to protect them from the brunt of the whirlwinds roaring inside the church.

Nikolai felt Mae's spell take root deep inside his core. The voices and pictures inside his head abated, along with the agony they had brought. He took a shaky breath and clung to her, grateful for her warmth.

His body felt like ice.

Alastair swayed on his shoulder, feathers drooping in pain. Nikolai touched him with trembling fingers.

The roof tore off with a sound that seemed to herald the end of days.

"Shit!" Mae cursed.

Bricks and wooden beams crashed down into the church and atop them. Her barrier held.

Nikolai's heart stuttered when she stiffened against him. He followed her stare to where the roof had been. His eyes rounded.

The clouds above them rippled before parting violently, as if struck by a powerful detonation. They thinned and vanished in an outward radiating circle, leaving a vapid sun pouring down upon the land from a pale blue sky.

The floor started trembling beneath Nikolai and Mae.

Brimstone snarled, snatched them up in his jaws by their jackets, and bounded out of the church, Hellreaver humming angrily beside him while Alastair kept pace above them.

The demon fox didn't stop until he reached the bottom of the hill.

A sickening magic filled the air as he lowered them to the ground. He whirled around and took up a defensive stance in front of them.

Nikolai shared a stunned look with Mae. "What's going on?!"

"I—I don't know!"

Warmth bloomed in his gut as she augmented *Soul Shield*.

"*My witch*," Brimstone growled in warning.

They followed the fox's glare.

"Oh God," Mae croaked.

Something was happening to the church and the hill. Something impossible.

The building and the elevation it stood upon started to vibrate at an impossible speed. Both blurred and vanished before their eyes seconds later, the whoosh that accompanied their disappearance almost mocking as they faded to nothingness.

They sat in the steaming mud and stared at the empty patch of dirt and grassland where the church and the hill had once stood.

CHAPTER THIRTEEN

AN OMINOUS FEELING GREW INSIDE MAE AS THEY DROVE away from Marblehead. She couldn't help but feel that they'd just fallen into the Dark Council's trap. Judging from the unease she could feel throbbing across her bond with Brimstone and Hellreaver, they shared her sentiments.

Mae only dimly recalled what had happened in those fleeting seconds when she'd lost control of her body. All she remembered was a woman's voice inside her head whispering that she should touch the dark sphere above the obsidian block. She hadn't been able to fight it, despite Brimstone and Nikolai's intervention.

One thing she was certain of. Whatever spell it was she'd triggered when she'd touched that globe hadn't been black magic.

Nikolai glanced at her as he changed gears, his knuckles white on the steering wheel. "Still can't get through?"

"No." Mae chewed her lip and stared at her cell. She couldn't raise Bryony or Abraham. "It keeps saying their numbers are unreachable."

Nikolai passed her his phone. "Try mine."

He stepped on the gas, his frowning gaze focused on the rain-lashed highway.

By the time they made it back to New York, Mae still hadn't been able to contact the New York coven. Brimstone stirred when they drove inside the underground garage beneath the headquarters on Madison Avenue. He jumped on Mae's lap, his ears cocking to and fro.

"What is it?" she said warily.

The fox's eyes flared crimson. *Something feels... different.*

Nikolai pulled up in an empty parking bay. They exited the SUV and hurried across the garage to the elevators.

"That's weird." The sorcerer looked around. "There sure are a lot of vehicles around for a Saturday night."

Mae eyed the full bays with a frown. Her dread deepened when she recalled how brightly lit the building had been when they were approaching it. She cast *Nullify*. It returned nothing.

Brim, do you smell black magic in the area?

No, my witch. He brushed her leg. *But there is a wrongness around us I cannot define.*

They stepped out on the first floor a moment later.

Nikolai rocked to a stop. "What the—?!"

A low growl rose from the depths of Brimstone's chest.

The interior of the headquarters looked different. And it wasn't just the decor that had changed appearance. The vibe of the place had transformed too. The air felt thicker. More sinister.

A group of sorcerers and witches came through the revolving doors of the main entrance. Brimstone's hackles rose.

"Fuck," Nikolai mumbled.

Mae's stomach churned as she observed the faint aura of darkness around their heads. It wasn't the same as that manifested by humans who'd been possessed by demons. But it contained a taint of power that reminded her eerily of the dark globe she had touched inside the church.

The sorcerers and witches rocked to a halt when they spotted Mae and Nikolai. Alarm widened their eyes.

"Hey, isn't that—?" one of them started.

Mae didn't wait for the rest of their question. She took Nikolai's hand and pulled him across the vestibule. "Let's get to Bryony's office."

They ignored the rising murmurs of the sorcerers and witches and made their way rapidly to the private elevator at the rear of the foyer. The woman who sat behind the reception desk in the lobby on the top floor wasn't someone Mae recognized. But she seemed to know Mae. Her face twisted with loathing.

"*Witch Queen!*" she spat.

A pale spell bomb flared into life in her right hand as she jumped to her feet. She hit a button beneath her desk and backed into the hallway leading to the coven's official meeting chambers and Bryony and Abraham's office, her dog familiar growling at her side.

An alarm started blaring inside the building. Mae flinched and looked around. She caught movement out of the corner of her eye.

The witch had cast her spell bomb at her.

Devour flared wordlessly into life above Mae's fingers. It swallowed the magic missile in an instant.

Brimstone bared his fangs. *How dare she?!*

"What is the meaning of this?" Nikolai snapped. "Why are you attacking us?!"

The woman's expression turned chagrined. She bowed briskly. "I apologize, Master Nikolai." She glared at Mae. "This evil witch has cast a powerful enchantment upon you. Please, come with me. We can help you regain your senses!"

Mae and Nikolai exchanged a startled glance.

Master?! Mae's heart thudded against her ribs as she tried to make sense of the woman's words.

My witch! Brimstone warned.

The fox shifted into his nine-tailed form just as a volley of powerful spell bombs arrowed toward them. Hellreaver transformed and sliced through half a dozen of the attacks. Crimson detonated around Brimstone, his vibrating tails casting a whirlwind that diverted the rest across the lobby.

The spell bombs smashed into a bay of windows. Glass exploded.

Nikolai raised a Moon Magic barrier at the same

time Mae drew a shield around them. The glittering fragments filling the air bounced harmlessly off the protective walls.

The sinister foreboding that had been building inside Mae on the ride over here from Marblehead bloomed into an ice-cold conviction that shook her to the core as she stared at the witch and sorcerer who had just attacked her.

"Master Nikolai, step away from that enchantress," Bryony ground out.

Penley hissed at her feet, the black cat's pupils blazing jade with magic.

Abraham glowered at Mae. "We shall apprehend Mae Jin and force her to break her wicked spell on you. Come to us, my liege. We mean you no harm."

He extended a hand toward Nikolai.

Nikolai's watch extended into a spear. Hellfire licked at his skin.

"I don't know what's happening here, but there is no way in hell I'm coming with you," the sorcerer growled. "You better explain why you're so intent on—!"

"They don't remember." Mae's nails bit into her palms. She met Nikolai's shocked stare. "They don't know who I am."

Though she couldn't fathom the name nor the nature of the magic she had set off in the church in Marblehead Neck, its intention was now horrifyingly clear.

Bryony scoffed. "Of course we know who you are. You're the demon witch who has ensnared our future

Sorcerer King in her trap." Her fingers tightened on the handle of her sword. "Give up, Mae Jin. He will never be yours and neither will his throne!"

Nikolai paled. "What?!"

Mae swallowed, her mind racing. *They believe Nikolai is the next Sorcerer King?!*

"It would seem so, my witch," Brimstone growled. *"They appear to have fallen for the Dark Council's trick."*

"It isn't a trick," Mae said between clenched teeth.

"What?" Nikolai mumbled.

She met his confused gaze and that of the fox, her pulse racing. "That strange storm and the wave that washed across the sky when we were in the church? It was some kind of spell. It's altered their memories of us." She paused as she recalled how the foyer of the building had looked different. She narrowed her eyes. "And our own to a certain extent."

Dread darkened his face as the meaning behind her words sank in.

Mae widened her stance and reached for her magic. "Right now, the only people in this building who recall the true reality of our circumstances and our war with the Sorcerer King are the two of us."

"Shit," Nikolai mumbled.

I have never heard of such a conjuration, my witch, Hellreaver rumbled.

Brimstone made a troubled sound. *"Neither have I."*

Mae's emotions warred inside her as she observed Bryony and Abraham. On the one hand, she had no option but to defend herself if they kept on attacking her. On the other, she didn't want to hurt them.

That choice was taken out of her hands when the elevator doors opened. Sorcerers and witches spilled out of the cabin and surrounded them, weapons raised and spell bombs at the ready.

"Do not harm Master Nikolai," Bryony ordered coldly. "Feel free to take down the demon."

The coven witches and sorcerers prepared to cast their attacks.

Mae gritted her teeth. *Damn it!*

Whiteness flared beside her.

"*Moon Storm!*" Nikolai growled.

The air shivered on the pale wave he unleashed, his magic causing Mae's core to throb in resonance. Her would-be attackers went flying across the lobby. Bryony and Abraham cursed when they were shoved back some dozen feet behind the defensive barriers they'd raised. Tremors shook the building.

"Let's get out of here!" Mae snapped.

Nikolai nodded. They bolted for the fire door to their right, Moon Storm keeping their friends-turned-enemies at bay. It opened just as they reached it.

Violet and Miles stepped inside the reception.

Mae's belly twisted as she stumbled to a halt. *No!*

"*It is alright, my witch,*" Brimstone rumbled. "*I do not sense malice from them.*"

Violet looked past Mae. Purple magic exploded in her hands and in her rabbit familiar Trixie's eyes.

A muscle ticked in Miles's cheek. "Looks like we're just in time."

Golden spheres bloomed in the sorcerer's hands. His boa constrictor Millie gave Mae a friendly hiss.

"I'm sorry about this, Aunt Bryony, Abraham." Violet stepped around Mae and Nikolai and took up a defensive stance, her gaze locked on the New York coven High Priestess and her aide. "But you guys are being misled by a powerful spell right now. Mae is not your enemy."

Relief stormed through Mae at the witch's words, leaving her weak. She didn't know why Violet and Miles were immune to the magic that had affected everyone else, but she was eternally grateful for it. Having to fight her closest friends would have haunted her for a long time.

Bryony's mouth pressed into a thin line. "I don't know what you're doing, Violet, but that woman is—!"

"Don't waste your breath," Abraham interrupted nastily. "It seems those two have become that demon's pawns."

"Our car's in front." Miles lobbed keys at Nikolai. "We'll meet up at your place. Vlad should be making his way over to your apartment."

Mae's heart throbbed. "Is he—?!"

"He's an incubus." Violet stretched out the kinks in her neck and cracked her knuckles as she assessed the sorcerers and witches preparing to charge. "This kind of magic won't work on him. Now, go!"

Mae swallowed and nodded. She and Nikolai dashed into the stairwell. *Wind Fury* and *Moon Storm* took care of the coven sorcerers and witches whose paths they crossed, while Hellreaver and Brimstone kept their angry familiars at bay.

They found Miles and Violet's SUV parked opposite

the main entrance, jumped inside the vehicle, and took off at lightning speed.

"There's somewhere we need to go first," Mae told Nikolai grimly as he tore down Madison Avenue.

He met her tense gaze and nodded.

CHAPTER FOURTEEN

THE HOUSE IN FLUSHING WAS JUST AS MAE REMEMBERED it. The scent of roses and wisteria tickled her nostrils when she stopped outside her front gate.

Lights were on in the downstairs hall and in Ye-Seul's bedroom. She scanned the driveway. Ryu's car was parked in its usual spot, as was her mother's old Honda.

"Are you sure you want to do this?" Nikolai said quietly.

Mae nodded. She already suspected what she would find if she were to knock on her front door right now. But still, she could not help herself. She had to know for certain.

The gate squeaked when she pushed it open. Nikolai trailed in her wake as she walked up to the house. She took her spare key out of her jeans, hesitated, and put it back in her pocket.

Mae stopped in front of the door and took a deep breath.

Brimstone brushed against her leg. Nikolai moved closer. Their presence gave her the courage she needed. She raised a hand and pressed the bell.

Footsteps sounded inside the house a moment later. A hazy figure appeared through the glazed glass making up the top section of the entrance.

Her father opened the door.

Mae's mind went blank.

A puzzled half-smile curved Han Tae Jin's lips as he observed them. "Yes? May I help you?"

"Dad?" Mae mumbled hoarsely. She raked his figure with her gaze, unable to believe the false reality before her eyes. "Is that—is that really you?!"

Her father didn't look a day older than when he'd died three years ago.

Nikolai drew a sharp breath. He grasped her shoulder, his touch as much a warning not to fall for the spell's untruths as it was a comfort to her. She gripped his fingers tightly, her vision blurring with tears.

Her father's expression grew awkward. "I'm sorry, I think you have the wrong address."

Brimstone whined when he sensed Mae's distress. Hellreaver trembled against her chest, similarly upset.

"Honey, is everything okay?"

Sorrow squeezed Mae's chest as Yoo-Mi popped out of the kitchen.

Her mother gave her and Nikolai a puzzled look before wiping her hands on a kitchen towel and coming over.

"Who is this?" she asked her husband curiously.

Mae's nails sank into the back of Nikolai's hand, the agony of the deception being played out in that moment so deep she wanted to shout and curse.

"We need to go," the sorcerer said softly.

Alastair crooned on his shoulder.

They're right, my witch, Brimstone murmured wretchedly. *There is nothing to be gained by being here.*

Mae inhaled shakily. It took a few seconds to regain control of her emotions. "I'm sorry to have troubled you." She flashed a fake smile at her parents. "It seems we do have the wrong address after all. Goodnight."

She turned on her heels and left before they could utter a word, her fists clenched so tightly in her pockets she almost drew blood.

She'd known from the moment Nikolai had driven into the street that the magic she had inadvertently unleashed had affected her family too. The houses the New York coven had bought a few months ago to place Noah Tegner and his protection team in position to guard Yoo-Mi, Ryu, and Ye-Seul blazed with light and her old neighbors' cars were parked on their respective drives once more.

Nikolai caught up with her next to the SUV.

"I know this is going to sound crass, but are you okay?" he asked worriedly.

The sob Mae had been holding back finally tumbled from her lips. He clenched his jaw and took her in his arms wordlessly. Mae clung to him as he cradled her head against his shoulder, her hot tears soaking into his leather jacket.

They stood like that for a long time, Nikolai gently

stroking her hair while Hellreaver and their familiars kept a watch out for their enemy.

Mae finally shuddered and pulled back.

Nikolai handed her a tissue. She blew her nose noisily.

"I'm gonna crush your father's balls when I find him," she said darkly. "I hope you don't mind."

Nikolai blinked. A snort left him.

"I don't," he chuckled. "I'll even serve them to you on a platter."

Mae smiled weakly. He startled when she touched his cheek.

His expression sobered. "What?"

Mae swallowed, the emotions swirling inside her strong enough to choke her breath all over again.

"I'm glad you didn't forget about me," she whispered. "I don't know what I would do if you had."

Her confession made Nikolai's gaze heat up. He slipped a hand around the back of her head and pulled her in for a torrid kiss. Mae melted into him, eager for the passion that blazed so easily between them. It eased her mind and warmed her ice-cold soul.

Nikolai reluctantly ended the kiss. He pressed his forehead against Mae, his skin so hot it almost scorched her flesh.

He took her hand. "Let's go home."

Mae nodded, her fingers tightening around his.

But the apartment wasn't there when they got to Ridgewood, nor the movie theater it stood above. In their stead was a modern office building. Mae's stomach plummeted as they got out of the vehicle and stared at the edifice across the road, Nikolai's face reflecting her disquiet.

It looked like it had been there for years.

This is still an illusion, right?!

I suspect so, my witch. Brimstone growled. *I can still smell your scent coming from that building.*

"Mae!" someone called out.

They whirled around. Vlad was jogging up the street toward them, Tarang loping at his side.

Mae's eyes widened when she saw the figure with them.

She gasped as Vlad took her in his arms and lifted her off her feet. His heart pounded violently against her chest as he embraced her, his body quivering with tension. She hugged him back just as tightly.

Brimstone and Tarang greeted one another with anxious rumbles.

The incubus finally let her go. "What the hell is going on?" His brow furrowed as he looked from Mae to Nikolai. "I got this crazy phone call from Violet. She wasn't making any sense. She said something about the New York coven coming after you! Is it the work of the Dark Council?!"

Mae didn't answer right away.

She stared at Cortes, her pulse racing. "You remember who I am?"

The Columbian nodded grimly. Popo ruffled his feathers uneasily on his sorcerer's shoulder.

"I helped Enrique resist that weird magic," the parrot mumbled. "It was a close call, though. If I hadn't been in the room with him at the time, we would have been in trouble."

Vlad stared. "What weird magic?"

Cortes observed their surroundings warily. "It might be best to have this conversation somewhere else. Right now, everyone you used to consider an ally should be treated as a potential enemy until proven—"

Tires screeched in the distance, drowning out the rest of his words. A battered Volvo shot into the junction to the south, turned sharply, and barreled up the street toward them.

Vlad's eyes flashed crimson. Cortes unleashed his sword.

"It's okay," Mae said hastily.

The Volvo squealed to a stop next to them. The window wound down.

"We need to move," Violet said tensely from the driver's seat. "They're on our tail."

Miles was staring at the building on the corner. "What happened to your apartment?"

"It's an illusion," Mae said bitterly.

Vlad's expression grew pinched. "We should go to my place. Whoever it is that's after you won't be able to—"

The low hum of a scooter had their heads whipping around. It took a few seconds to figure out which direction it was coming from.

Mae's eyes rounded. *I know that sound!*

A green Vespa rounded the bend to their right.

Riding it was Mrs. Son-Ha. She was dressed in a thick purple coat, orange flannel pants, pink trainers, and wore the world's ugliest fanny pack strapped to her belly. Her Chihuahua Dexter sat in the front basket of the scooter, his gray muzzle poking out from under the hood of a hideous, yellow coat.

Mae gaped. "Bet—*Betsy?!*"

"Who's Betsy?" Cortes asked, nonplussed.

"Her Vespa," Nikolai mumbled.

Cortes looked at him dully. "She called her scooter Betsy?"

Popo shifted on the Columbian's shoulder. "That's a real ugly dog. Don't go near it, Enrique. It might contaminate your good looks."

Mrs. Son-Ha pulled up beside them.

"Don't think I didn't hear that, you bag of flea-infested feathers," she snapped at the parrot.

Dexter yipped.

"I—I don't have fleas!" Popo squawked, flapping his wings.

Mae finally recovered from the shock of seeing the gossip queen of Koreatown riding her trusty scooter. She blinked dazedly.

Things just keep getting weirder!

"What's going on? How come you have Betsy? And —" She stopped and swallowed, a singular truth resonating inside her. "Wait. You remember who I am?!"

"More to the point, she can see familiars," Violet commented warily.

"But—you're not a witch!" Mae blurted out at the old woman. "I can tell, since I can see magic cores. You don't have one."

"You make it sound like that's a weakness," Mrs. Son-Ha said sourly. She watched Mae for a moment, reached inside her coat pocket, and passed her a red ginseng candy. "Here, you look like you could do with a pick-me-up. Follow me. My house is the safest place in this city right now for you people."

She pulled on the throttle of the Vespa and had traveled a good twenty feet before she realized they hadn't moved. She stopped and directed a scowl at them over her shoulder.

"Are you coming or not? I haven't got all night, you know."

CHAPTER FIFTEEN

MRS. SON-HA'S TWO-STORY CLAPBOARD HOUSE STOOD like an ominous sentinel at the end of a cul-de-sac in Glendale. They parked behind her Subaru, crossed an immaculately maintained front yard dotted with gnomes with fishing poles, and headed up a short flight of red-brick steps.

Nikolai scanned the dark street as they crowded under the covered porch. It was eerily quiet, even for a Saturday night.

"This place is deader than some of the graveyards I've visited," Cortes observed.

"Ditto," Vlad muttered.

Mrs. Son-Ha glanced at them as she fished her house keys out of her fanny pack. "There's a Mahjong competition at the local civic hall. Which is a good thing, considering your present circumstances. Those busybodies would have poked their noses in our business faster than you can bleed a stuck pig."

"Hey, didn't Mae say that old lady is the number one gossip on Long Island?" Miles whispered to Violet.

"Are all Korean matriarchs like this or is it just the people you know?" Cortes asked Mae.

A cacophony of excited barks and yips erupted inside the property when Mrs. Son-Ha opened the front door. Two Chihuahuas, three Shih Tzus, and something that like looked like a cross between a Jack Russell and a poodle shot out of a room off the main hallway and bolted toward them at lightning speed.

The dogs skidded comically on the hardwood floor at the sight of Tarang and Brimstone. They hesitated before approaching with cautious sniffs, their tails down. Dexter yipped confidently in Mrs. Son-Ha's arms. She released the Chihuahua and took his coat off. Lines wrinkled her brow when she turned and saw them hovering on the doorstep.

"What are you waiting for, an official invitation?" she snapped.

They reluctantly crowded inside the hallway.

Mrs. Son-Ha peeked out at the sky and shivered. "Jeez, it's not even October yet and it's already cold enough to freeze the balls off a brass monkey out there. This winter is gonna be a killer."

She shut the door and locked it.

Nikolai exchanged a cautious glance with Mae while the old lady engaged two more deadbolts.

Mrs. Son-Ha placed her house keys on a hook on the wall and pointed at their feet.

"Shoes off," she ordered imperiously. "Coats go on the rack." Her gaze dropped to Tarang and Brimstone.

She squinted. "You two are dead meat if you poop in the house."

The tiger and the fox huffed, affronted.

"I should talk her into working for the *Black Devils*," Vlad told Cortes.

"I know what you mean," the Columbian agreed. "It's like her voice is wired to my hindbrain."

"You have a sharp mouth on you, young man." Mrs. Son-Ha studied Cortes with a shrewd look. Her gaze shifted to Mae. "You should make him your consort. He has good genes. I see beautiful children in his future."

Nikolai clenched his jaw. Vlad's eyes glowed red.

Mae clocked their thunderous faces.

"I think I'll pass on that," she said glassily.

"I knew it!" Popo bobbed excitedly on Cortes's shoulder. "I said you had good seeds, Enrique. How about we—*mmph, mmph!*"

Cortes muzzled his filthy-mouthed familiar and fixed Mrs. Son-Ha with a penetrating stare. "You can see my future?"

The old lady shrugged. "I see the possibilities of several futures for each of you." Her gaze flicked to Nikolai. "It doesn't mean any of it will come to pass, though."

Nikolai couldn't help but feel that she'd just given him some kind of warning.

Mae lifted her chin, her tone growing defiant. "Who are you, really? Also, how come there's a divine barrier around your house?"

Nikolai startled. Vlad blinked.

Violet exchanged a stunned look with Miles. "Is that what that is?!"

"I felt something familiar out on the drive, but I didn't realize it's a barrier," her cousin muttered, troubled.

"I should think it's familiar. It's the reason that magic didn't work on you." Mrs. Son-Ha's mouth twisted into a cunning half-smile. "But you should know that, since *she* already told you."

Mae stared, confused. "She?"

"Our ally in Chicago," Violet said awkwardly.

"She contacted us and told us we had to return to New York," Miles explained.

"What's a divine barrier?" Cortes arched an eyebrow. "And who's this person in Chicago you're talking about?"

"How about we take this conversation to the kitchen?" Mrs. Son-Ha grumbled. "I'm not as young as I used to be and my legs are hurting from all this standing around. I'll make you some hot cocoa."

"We're a bit old for hot cocoa," Mae remarked.

Mrs. Son-Ha narrowed her eyes. "You're gonna have the hot cocoa and you're gonna enjoy it, young lady."

"Yes, ma'am," Mae mumbled hastily.

"I'm in half a mind to invite her to the cartel myself," Cortes told Vlad.

They followed the old lady to the back of the house. The kitchen was surprisingly cozy and devoid of dog smells. Mae waited until Mrs. Son-Ha finished making their drinks before asking the question on everyone's lips.

"If you're not a witch, then how come you didn't fall under the Dark Council's spell?"

Mrs. Son-Ha grimaced. "Dark Council? Sheesh, talk about an original name." She took a careful sip of her cocoa and waved a hand around. "The barrier around this house is pretty strong. Besides, I have a number of spirits protecting me from external influences." Her narrow-eyed gaze landed on Hellreaver where he was exploring the kitchen. "That thing had better not break anything."

Hellreaver flinched and silently returned to Mae's side.

"Spirits?" Nikolai asked skeptically.

Vlad grimaced. "You mean, ghosts?"

Miles looked around the room nervously.

"Ghosts, spirits." Mrs. Son-Ha shrugged. "Call them what you want. As a Shaman, I can communicate with them and earn their protection."

"A Shaman?" Cortes said carefully.

"But Alicia said ghosts don't exist," Mae protested.

Mrs. Son-Ha stared. "Who's Alicia?"

"She's the Queen of Soul Reapers." Nikolai hesitated. "She did mention something about the lingering remains of the dead."

"Queen of Soul Reapers, huh?" Mrs. Son-Ha grew thoughtful. "I'd like to meet her one day. And she's correct, of course. What I'm talking about are the remnants of souls that have clung to our realm." She leveled a steady stare at Cortes. "I'm sure they have Shamans in your country. And, from what I can see around you, this wasn't your first time encountering that nasty spell either."

Cortes's shoulders tightened. "What do you mean?"

Mrs. Son-Ha ignored his deadly tone and frowned at something on his left. Her face grew unfocused. "It looks like it was some time ago. And it appears you lost someone precious as a result."

Surprise widened Cortes's eyes.

"Wait," Mae mumbled in a strained voice. She met the Columbian's shocked gaze. "Is she talking about when Raya killed your familiar and cracked your core?!"

Tension thrummed through Nikolai. Few people outside their circle and Cortes's coven knew what Raya Medeiros had done to the sorcerer when he was a teen. The old woman's next words sent a chill down his spine and made Mae pale.

"The magic that erased everyone's recollections of who Mae is tonight, and that was used on your friend in the past, is a mirage," Mrs. Son-Ha said in a measured voice. "It distorts the memories of the people it affects. Even I am not immune to it. Although I am certain your apartment is still there, it doesn't appear that way to me."

Mae's jaw tightened. "So, my father hasn't really come back to life?"

Vlad gasped. "What?!"

"We went to Mae's home after we left the coven headquarters tonight," Nikolai explained in a hard voice. "Her father opened the door. He didn't know who Mae was and neither did her mom." He glanced at Mae. "We're pretty sure what we saw was an illusion."

"Shit." Violet's knuckles whitened on the table. "That's low."

Something that looked like sympathy filled Mrs. Son-Ha's eyes as she observed Mae. "I'm sorry."

CHAPTER SIXTEEN

Cortes stared unseeingly at his hands, his face ashen. "Is that why my family acted like that at the time Raya attacked me?" He looked up at them, his expression turning wild. "I knew something had changed. I could feel it in the way they looked at me, like I was some kind of parasite that had crawled out from under a rock. And they were all too eager to abandon me to my fate after my core cracked."

A fraught hush followed.

"Did your family ever try to make amends?" Mrs. Son-Ha said, her tone not unkind.

A muscle jumped in Cortes's jawline. "They did some time after the incident, but by then I was already in the cartel's line of sight. Truth be told, I couldn't trust their words." A mirthless laugh left him. "Now that my core is healed and I've subjugated our coven, all their attempts to approach me feel like the efforts of desperate people trying to cling to power."

Mae's heart ached as she looked at the Columbian. Popo crooned worriedly on his sorcerer's shoulder.

Mrs. Son-Ha drummed her fingers on the table.

"I believe your family is still trying to make amends," she told Cortes curtly. "They must have been as shocked as you were after they recovered from the effects of that magic. You should listen to what they have to say." She paused, as if listening to something. Her expression relaxed a little. "It seems that dove has been keeping watch over you all these years. She's happy you found another familiar."

Cortes blanched. "You can see Della?!"

Mae blinked. *Is Della the name of his dead familiar?*

A sad sound left Brimstone. *It seems so.*

"No. The other spirits told me." Mrs. Son-Ha cut her eyes to Popo. "He's a strong one and more than a match for you."

For once, Popo didn't come up with any smart repartee. He inched closer to Cortes and pressed his body against his neck in an attempt to comfort him. Cortes touched the familiar gently, his face haggard.

"The magic you wield can protect you against this mirage spell," Mrs. Son-Ha said. "I suspect whoever attacked you with it the first time didn't realize this."

"How do you know all of this?" Suspicion darkened Violet's eyes. "I've never even heard of that magic and I was born in a family of witches and sorcerers."

"She's right," Mae said, equally troubled. "When I awakened as the Witch Queen, I inherited a repository of spells Azazel and Ran Soyun had taught their daughter Na Ri, my original incarnation. I've never seen magic like this."

"Hmm." Mrs. Son-Ha rubbed her chin thoughtfully. "He did tell me it was rare."

The rest of them traded confused glances.

"Who told you it was rare?" Mae said cautiously.

"The guy who sold me this." Mrs. Son-Ha rose, shuffled over to the sink, and picked up an antique dragon bell from the windowsill. She brought it over to the kitchen table. "I got it from a shop in Hong Kong, years ago. The man who owned the place said it would create a divine barrier in the presence of a spiritual or demonic attack and would be of use to me in the future." She grunted. "Of course, I just thought he was a charlatan at the time. But as my Shaman powers grew, I could tell this thing wasn't normal."

Mae's pulse quickened as she stared at the object. She could feel an otherworldly power throbbing from it. It tasted similar to the shimmering, golden light Violet and Miles occasionally manifested.

From Nikolai's surprised expression, he could sense it too.

"Hong Kong?" Violet repeated in a suspicious tone.

Miles startled as if he'd recalled something. He shot a shocked look at his cousin. "Isn't that where Haruki's brother got those prayer beads?!"

Violet's mouth flattened into a thin line. "I'm pretty sure we were supposed to keep that under wraps, dumbass."

Miles shifted guiltily under her accusing gaze.

Vlad furrowed his brow. "Who's Haruki?"

Miles scratched his cheek. "Um, he's one of the divine beasts we told you about before."

Violet sighed. "He wields the Flaming Sword of Camael, a holy artifact."

Brimstone raised his head from where he'd been lying by Mae's chair. *Camael?*

Mae detected his surprise across their bond. "Do you know him?"

Brimstone huffed. *Yes. He's one of Azazel's old companions.*

"Really?" Mae said dubiously.

"What did he say?" Vlad asked.

"Apparently, Camael is an archangel and one of my father's friends."

Nikolai grimaced. "You're saying an archangel set up a shop in Hong Kong?"

Violet shuddered. "You'd be surprised what those lunatics get up to."

Mrs. Son-Ha squinted. "That guy looked like he needed a shave. And a bath."

Cortes studied Violet and Miles with a leaden expression. "More to the point, you guys know archangels?"

Violet hesitated.

"The only ones we've officially met are Michael and Uriel," she confessed reluctantly. "Although, technically, Otis is a seraph too."

"Otis?" A memory danced through Mae. "Oh, you mean Mila's boyfriend?"

Mila Jackson was an Immortal they'd met in Philadelphia, along with Madeleine Godard-Black.

Both women were renowned scientists in their respective fields and had helped them identify Dietrich Farago's abominable, parasitic creation: an artificial virus infused with Barquiel's demonic DNA, black magic, and, eventually, Mae's blood. It had allowed the ghouls Barquiel had recruited from Hell to possess the Philadelphia coven sorcerers and witches the Dark Council had kidnapped and enter the *Book of Light* so as to turn it into its true form: a compass that could lead to the *Book of Shadows*.

Mae stared blindly at the table as the pieces of the puzzle started to fall in place.

If an archangel sold Mrs. Son-Ha that artifact years ago because he knew it would eventually help us, then everything's connected.

Yes, Brimstone agreed. *It is becoming clear that that is the case, my witch.*

Her pulse quickened as she looked at Mrs. Son-Ha. "Did he tell you the name of this magic or how to counter it?"

The old woman shook her head, dashing her hopes. "Alas, no. I get the feeling he only caught a glimpse of that particular future himself."

"Same as our friend in Chicago," Violet admitted. "She can see several futures. Which one turns out to be our true destiny is always guided by our actions in the present."

Mae worried her lip with her teeth, unease twisting her insides as a fresh realization resonated inside her.

"What is it?" Nikolai said tensely.

"The magic I unleashed today did not taste of the Dark Council's corruption."

Vlad leaned his elbows on the table, his expression growing focused. "Tell us exactly what happened. And don't skip any details."

Mae and Nikolai related how the Boston coven had gotten in touch with Bryony and why they'd been the ones who'd ended up going to Marblehead Neck.

A muscle ticked in Vlad's jawline when they described what had taken place inside the church. Mrs. Son-Ha narrowed her eyes. Cortes's face darkened.

"The whole place disappeared?!" Violet gasped.

"Like the entire hill and the church?" Miles said in disbelief.

They grew more perturbed when Mae described how Bryony and Abraham had referred to Nikolai during the attack she had been subjected to at the New York coven headquarters.

"They believe you're the future Sorcerer King?" Cortes asked the sorcerer.

Nikolai nodded, discomfited.

"I can only think of one reason behind all of this." Mae clenched her jaw, the suspicion that had been roused inside her in the last few hours solidifying into a cold certitude. She met Nikolai's worried gaze. "Vedran is trying to capture you."

"Though I do not know the details of how covens work, I find it surprising that your boss decided to send you to that church," Mrs. Son-Ha told Nikolai suspiciously. "It sounded like a job well beneath your abilities."

Mae startled. *She's right.*

Nikolai scowled. "She said they asked for a white magic user. Does that mean someone in the Boston coven is working for the Dark Council?"

"Not necessarily." Mae's mouth flattened to a thin line. "They may have been influenced to do so."

"Or had the suggestion implanted in their mind." Cortes studied Mae with a pensive frown. "More to the point, you seem to be forgetting something. I agree it looks like the Dark Council are trying to get their hands on the trump card that escaped them," he glanced at Nikolai, "but there's something even more important at play here."

Mae stared. "There is?"

Realization brought a scowl to Violet's face. "Shit."

"You, Mae," Cortes said quietly. "What good is a Witch Queen if her people not only forget she exists, but consider her their number one enemy?"

Crimson flared in Vlad's eyes. "Those assholes!"

Brimstone and Hellreaver made angry sounds.

Mae's stomach plummeted, the truth of Cortes's words echoing through her mind. *Oh God! Why didn't I think of that?!*

Nikolai met her shocked gaze, his face ashen.

"They're right," he mumbled. "If we don't break this spell, then my father and Barquiel might as well have won this war before it's even begun. No one in the magic community will believe us or take our side. And we cannot defeat the Dark Council on our own."

CHAPTER SEVENTEEN

MAE WOKE UP TO A HOT TONGUE LAPPING enthusiastically at her face. She groaned and pushed at the furry body sitting on her chest.

"We need to do something about your morning breath, Brim."

That's not me.

Mae's eyes slammed open. Dexter yipped excitedly and resumed his ablutions where he crouched atop her. She carefully lifted the excited dog and sat up, the blankets pooling at her waist.

Violet's spot beside her in the bed in Mrs. Son-Ha's spare room was empty. From the coolness of the sheets, she'd been gone a while.

They're downstairs having breakfast, Brimstone said distractedly.

The fox had his paws up on the windowsill and was staring outside with Hellreaver.

Mae stiffened, her belly warming as she reached for her magic. "Is everything okay?"

Brimstone huffed. *Do not worry, my witch. It's not that we sense an impending attack. It's just...the wrongness around us deepens with every passing hour.*

We have to reverse this spell and soon, Hellreaver said anxiously. *Before your existence is erased for good.*

The crushing dread that had gripped her last night and that had only abated with sleep surged afresh inside Mae. By the time she headed downstairs, her gut was tight with tension.

Mrs. Son-Ha looked up from where she was emptying sausages and eggs from a frying pan onto Cortes's plate.

"There you are." She narrowed her eyes. "Anyone tell you you sleep like the dead?"

Mae's stomach grumbled loudly before she could come up with a reply.

Mrs. Son-Ha rolled her eyes. She indicated the steaming pot on the table. "Have some tea while I make you breakfast." Her sharp gaze dropped to Brimstone and Hellreaver. "There's steak and bacon for you two over there. You better hurry up and eat your share before the tiger steals it all."

Tarang looked up guilty from where he was attacking a veritable mountain of meat piled on a dish on the floor. He licked his chops and made space for Brimstone and Hellreaver to join him.

Mae pulled up a chair between Nikolai and Vlad. "You guys sleep okay?"

Mrs. Son-Ha had given them sleeping bags for the night and told them to use the couch and armchair in her sitting room.

Nikolai scowled. "No. Some asshole kept kicking me."

Vlad looked at him innocently. "I'm telling you I have restless legs."

Cortes shrugged at Mae's questioning look. "I took the couch."

"I slept like a baby," Miles confessed sheepishly.

"Both you and Mae could sleep through a goddamn earthquake," Violet muttered.

Mrs. Son-Ha sat down with them a short while later. Mae looked guiltily from her greasy breakfast to the old woman's bowl of porridge.

"Don't mind me," their host said at her expression. "You have to look after your health when you get to my age."

Mae hesitated before tucking enthusiastically into her food. She'd demolished half her plate when she paused, fork poised above a sausage. A sudden thought had just come to her. She swallowed the mouthful of eggs she'd just taken and studied Mrs. Son-Ha warily.

"By the way, does this mean you saw what happened at Mr. Ho-Nam's funeral?"

Wang Ho-Nam was an elderly patriarch who had passed on some two months ago. His funeral had been held at Mae's family-run funeral home and had been the most attended in Koreatown in a decade. This hadn't been so much because he was a well-respected and revered member of the community, as it had been for the spectacle likely to unfold when his wife Kyo Seung Ho-Nam and his mistress Jang-Mi Ye'un's warring families inevitably clashed at his final rites.

To no one's surprise, the funeral had descended into anarchy after someone threw a box of incense at Jang-Mi Ye'un's head. It was thanks to Mrs. Son-Ha that things hadn't escalated enough for the cops to be called.

The old woman blinked. She cackled in the next instant, her shoulders shaking. "I'd forgotten about that. The look on your face when you saw the boa constrictor was priceless."

Millie looked up guiltily from where she was eating fruit with Trixie, Alastair, and Popo.

Vlad grimaced at Mae. "Wasn't that the incident where you got punched?"

Cortes raised an eyebrow. "Someone punched her?"

"One of the widows," Nikolai muttered.

Mae pursed her lips and eyed their host accusingly.

"Oh, come now," Mrs. Son-Ha chortled. "Allow an old woman her fun once in a while." She stopped laughing and sighed. "It's a shame my foolish son didn't inherit his father's charisma. Ryu would have made a lovely daughter-in-law."

Mae made a face at that.

"She tried to hook Ryu up with her son?!" Violet hissed out of the corner of her mouth.

"Yeah." Mae studied Mrs. Son-Ha warily. "Have you always known? That I'm a witch?"

Mrs. Son-Ha waved a hand vaguely. "Not until your awakening unleashed that awful magic storm. That sure was a humdinger. All my spirits fled the city that day."

They all looked at Nikolai.

He frowned. "It couldn't be helped, alright?"

It wasn't until they'd finished breakfast that they finally got down to business.

"So, what's our game plan?" Vlad asked briskly.

Mae sighed and ran a hand through her hair. "I don't even know where to begin, to be honest."

Mrs. Son-Ha got up and started stacking the dishes. "I'll start on these while you guys chat. I don't think I'm going to be of any help to this conversation."

"Thank you," Mae murmured gratefully.

Violet rose. "I'll give you a hand."

She helped their host clear the table.

"Sergio Mendes's behavior and that of his coven at the reception still warrants investigation," Cortes said pensively. "He may know something about this mirage magic."

"I agree, although I still don't see the connection. The more I think about it, the more I'm convinced they were acting out of fear." Mae lowered her brows. "And I still don't get why the Dark Council instigated those two hellbeast attacks."

Mrs. Son-Ha turned on the small TV set on the counter and flicked through to a local news channel. The newscaster's voice and the running taps droned softly in the background. Violet returned to the table.

"Nothing stands out to you about those attacks?" the witch said. "Like, not even the smallest clue as to what they might have been after?"

"Not really," Mae confessed. "It all seemed pretty random."

Nikolai clenched his jaw. "The Dark Council

doesn't do anything without a motive. Violet is right. We must be missing something."

A wave of disquiet thrummed across Mae's bond with Brimstone. She looked around. Crimson trembled around the fox where he sat up dead straight next to Tarang.

Her mouth went dry at the dread in his eyes. "Brim?"

Your blood. Both of you were injured in those two fights, my witch. Demonic energy pulsed around him as he growled. *The sorcerer during the attack under our apartment and you at the reception. The wounds you incurred were minor, but you both bled!*

Mae's eyes rounded in horror. She knew instinctively that the fox was right.

Nikolai's nervous gaze swung between her and Brimstone. "What is it?"

The dots finally connected. Just like the time in Philadelphia when Barquiel and Farago had needed her blood to complete their evil experiment, the Dark Council had used her and Nikolai's blood for their current schemes.

"Our blood," she mumbled hoarsely. She stared at Nikolai. "You got scratched during the attack at the cinema. And Mendes's harpy eagle grazed my arm before she vanished." Mae swallowed. "I think they needed our blood to complete this mirage spell!"

Vlad cursed. A muscle twitched in Cortes's cheek.

Mrs. Son-Ha's grim voice made them all jump. "I hate to rain on what is already a shitty parade, but I'm afraid I have more bad news."

The old woman picked up the TV remote and turned up the volume.

Mae's breath stuttered when she saw her mugshot plastered across the screen. The voice of the newscaster registered dully in her ears above the blood pounding inside her skull.

"—terrorist behind the attack at the Paradise multiplex theater in Manhattan earlier this week and the Chateau Monteville on Friday night has been identified as one Hana Mae Jin. Her last known whereabouts are reported as Madison Avenue, late last night. Her hostage, Nikolai Stanisic, was also spotted at the time. It has emerged that Jin is behind other vicious attacks that have taken place in and around the city since summer. Be aware that Jin is deemed armed and dangerous and must not be approached under any circumstances. Please call the special number on the screen if you catch sight of her or Mr. Stanisic—"

Mrs. Son-Ha muted the volume.

Vlad jumped to his feet, his hands fisting at his sides. "What the hell?!"

Bile flooded the back of Mae's throat as a series of blurry witness videos started playing on the TV. They showed her attacking people at various locations. The ones from the hotel had her cutting people down indiscriminately with Hellreaver, her face unrecognizable in its rage.

Nikolai scowled. "Shit! Those fuckers even made fake clips!"

Violet scrolled through her phone.

"This is all over social media," she reported in a tight voice.

Cortes's voice rang coldly in the fraught silence. "Divide and conquer." He frowned at Mae. "Not only have they isolated you from your friends and allies, they've just made you the number one fugitive in the country." He paused. "This is gonna make it harder for you to move around."

Mae broke out in a cold sweat.

The shock and grief of the last day crashed over her all over again, a wave of darkness that threatened to swallow her whole. Brimstone whined and propped his front paws on her lap. He pressed his forehead to hers, his magic and demonic energy resonating with her own as he tried to comfort her. Hellreaver wormed his way into her arms, his blades vibrating.

Mae closed her eyes and hugged her weapon and familiar.

Despair turned to anger. Heat flared inside her. She gritted her teeth and fought back the explosion of wrath that threatened to burst from her core, knowing it would likely blast the room apart. Glass rattled around her.

"Mae!" Nikolai warned.

Mae blinked her eyes open. The air had turned crimson with her power.

Mrs. Son-Ha glared at her accusingly from near the ceiling, where she and Dexter levitated. Cortes grimaced as he clung upside down to the table. Violet and Miles's knuckles were white where they'd grasped the refrigerator, their bodies halfway out of their chairs.

Only Vlad and Nikolai still had their feet on the ground, barely at that.

Mae shuddered. It took all her will power to clamp down on her emotions.

The red haze faded.

Dexter tumbled into the sink with an alarmed yip as the gravity in the room returned to normal.

CHAPTER EIGHTEEN

THE SUN SHINING DOWN UPON THE EAST COAST SEEMED to mock Mae as Vlad's Bentley barreled up the highway. They were on their way to Marblehead Neck.

"Are you sure that's a good idea, princess?" Vlad had asked when she'd suggested they return to the scene of the incident that had triggered the mirage spell.

"I want to see if I can find a trace of that magic," Mae had replied grimly. "Besides, I doubt the Dark Council are expecting us to go there."

"How about you let me take over?" Nikolai sneered presently at the incubus from the back seat. "You drive like an old lady."

Vlad narrowed his eyes at the sorcerer in the rearview mirror. "It's my car, asshole. And we don't exactly want to attract the attention of highway patrol, hence why I'm keeping to the speed limit."

Nikolai scoffed. "You mean, it's the *Black Devils'* car."

Vlad's tone grew arctic. "Considering I pretty much own the *Black Devils,* I don't really see your point."

Mae clenched her jaw.

Vlad shot a mildly disapproving look at her. "You shouldn't do that. You'll wear down your teeth."

"You two are wearing down my patience!" she retorted.

Would you like me to bite them? Brimstone volunteered from the footwell.

Tarang lifted his head and made a worried sound where he'd draped himself across the back seat and Nikolai's lap.

"Your tiger is heavy," Nikolai complained.

Tarang huffed and licked his face.

To Mae's relief, the signs for Marblehead Neck soon flashed by. Her thoughts strayed to Cortes and the Nolan cousins. Cortes had returned to his hotel to question his coven about the people Raya Medeiros had had in her entourage around the time she attacked him all those years ago. To his relief, it seemed their Arcane Magic had protected them from the mirage spell too. Mae hoped it might help them find a name for the specific magic that had been used to alter his family's memories and maybe even the person who'd cast it.

Violet and Miles had accompanied them in their SUV as far as Boston before veering off and heading into the city. They were going to pay a discreet visit to the coven there and see if they could sniff out a clue.

Vlad exited the expressway a short while later. He drove through the sleepy town of Marblehead and crossed the isthmus leading to Marblehead Neck. Mae gave him directions to where she and Nikolai had come the day before. He slowed and carefully rolled onto the muddy track minutes later.

The incubus surveyed the deserted landscape with a faint frown. "This is something else."

"I'm pretty certain you've been to creepier places," Nikolai said nastily.

He cursed as Vlad deliberately drove into a pothole and sent his head bumping against the window. The incubus smirked.

Mae flashed a narrow-eyed look at them.

They parked where Nikolai had stopped his vehicle the day before and got out of the Bentley. Tension knotted the sorcerer's shoulders as they started across the empty lot where the hill and the church had stood. Vlad scanned their surroundings guardedly, crimson blooming in his eyes. Tarang brushed against his leg, the tiger's uneasy gaze sweeping the eerie scenery.

Bar the wind bringing the taste of salt off the ocean crashing against the cliffs and the pale seagulls whirling in the sunny sky, they were alone.

Brimstone scampered ahead of Mae as they neared the center of the plot. He stopped, ears pricking, and sniffed at the ground.

There is something here, my witch. It is very faint.

Mae joined him and studied the spot that had roused his interest.

"What is it?" Nikolai said warily.

"Brim says he can feel something here."

She squatted, pressed her hand to the dirt, and closed her eyes.

Her pulse quickened when she picked up on what Brimstone had detected with his nose.

I was right. There's a trace of that magic still here!

Her blood warmed as she drew on her powers. Hellreaver trembled against her chest.

"Reveal."

Nothing happened. Mae clenched her jaw and released even more of the potent energy that lived in her soul. The ground trembled slightly.

"REVEAL!"

Images flashed before her eyes with a suddenness that froze her breath.

A desolate, red plain with a forked tree. A hill with an abandoned church atop it that looked identical to the one that had stood in this very spot the day before. Winding, moss-covered, stone steps leading to a basement deep underground. And in the middle of a crypt, chained to an obsidian pillar that rose straight through the ceiling and brimmed with runes of blue fire, a woman with long, ash-blonde hair.

Blood caked her skin where she'd struggled against the manacles binding her wrists. She was on her knees, her head bowed and pain etched in every line of her quivering body.

Mae could tell her shoulders were dislocated.

Shadowy figures kept watch around the woman, their faces hidden beneath dark hoods. The air flickered around the altar and the woman. They were guarding her with some kind of shield.

Mae's heart clenched when the stranger's features came into view at an angle. She was beautiful, even in her agony.

The woman's head moved jerkily, as if she sensed Mae's stare. Her gray gaze locked onto Mae's with an eeriness that raised goosebumps on her flesh.

Mae's pulse stuttered. *Can she see me?!*

Blue flames filled the woman's pupils. They rounded with shock. Tears bloomed in her eyes and spilled down her grimy cheeks. Her expression crumpled with sorrow and regret.

Her cracked lips moved, forming words Mae didn't hear but felt in her very marrow.

I'm...sorry...!

"—e! —ae! Mae! *MAE!*"

Nikolai and Vlad's alarmed voices shattered the trance she'd fallen under. They were gripping her shoulders and trying to yank her back.

Mae lifted her fingers off the ground and fell on her behind. Air wheezed through her windpipe as she finally drew breath, the cold sea breeze filling her lungs and making her chest ache. Her heart thundered violently, the echoes of what she'd just seen still dancing before her eyes.

"What the hell happened just now?!" Vlad snapped.

Mae didn't answer him right away.

She looked wildly at Brimstone. "Did you see that?!"

The fox growled. *I did, my witch. I think that woman may be the one responsible for the magic you unleashed yesterday.*

Nikolai took hold of her elbow as she made to rise and helped her to her feet. "What did you see?"

His voice was hard and his eyes dark with dread as he looked from her to Brimstone.

Mae swallowed and described the vision they'd just had, if vision was even the right word for what had just transpired.

Nikolai and Vlad exchanged a troubled look.

"Are you sure it wasn't just some kind of—" the incubus paused and waved a hand vaguely, "I don't know, left-over hallucination from that magic?"

Mae met Brimstone's gaze. "No. We both saw the same thing." She looked at the two men, conviction settling inside her. "Brim thinks that woman is the one who created the mirage spell."

"So, it's a witch." A muscle ticked in Nikolai's cheek. "From what you saw, it seems she's a prisoner of the Dark Council. Do you have any idea where she's being held?"

Mae fisted her hands. "No."

A gust of wind whipped at their hair and clothes.

Vlad shivered. "Let's get out here for now."

They trooped inside the Bentley and were soon back on the expressway.

Halfway to Boston, the hum of rotors reached Mae's ears. She stiffened and looked out the window.

"You guys hear that?"

CHAPTER NINETEEN

Vlad's expression tightened. His gaze swept the sky to the left.

Nikolai drew a sharp breath in the back seat. "Behind us!"

Mae twisted around, the seat belt digging into her midriff. A black helicopter bearing the logo of the Massachusetts State Police was visible through the rear windshield. It swooped down toward them.

Vlad cursed and stepped on the gas. "How the hell did they find us?!"

Mae scowled. "It's probably the work of the Dark Council!"

Flashing light bars appeared amidst the traffic on the opposite highway as they rounded a bend. Half a dozen patrol cars shot past, sirens blaring. Tires screeched wildly moments later.

The cops were doing a U-turn where the concrete median gave way to amber center lines.

The civilian vehicles in their path slowed sharply as they hurtled down the highway after the Bentley.

"Looks like the cat is officially out of the bag." Nikolai watched the vehicles closing in on their tail, a muscle ticking in his jawline. "We're gonna have to lose them and fast!"

The helicopter's downdraft made the Bentley shudder as it darted overhead. Vlad swerved around a motorhome and straightened the car, his knuckles white on the steering wheel.

The aircraft turned up ahead and dropped to a low hover, nose facing them.

"Pull over!" someone shouted angrily over the loudspeakers. "We know you're harboring the fugitive Hana Mae Jin!"

Mae's eyes widened.

"Shit." Nikolai gripped the headrest of her seat, her shock reflected on his face. "Is that Jared?!"

"Looks like they're intending to ram us off the road!" Vlad snarled.

The helicopter was barely reversing as they closed in on it.

Gunfire erupted behind them. A bullet bounced off the tailgate of the Bentley. Another pinged off the rear windshield.

Hellfire magic bloomed around Nikolai. "I can't believe these assholes are shooting at us!"

"Don't worry." Vlad glanced at the rearview mirror and furrowed his brow. "My car has armor plating and bulletproof glass." He clenched his teeth. "Also, how about you not burn up my custom-made leather seats?!"

Movement in the sky to the right had Mae's head whipping around. Her nails dug into her palms. "Is your Bentley grenade proof?!"

Vlad swore colorfully when he saw the helicopter gunship flying in from the north.

"You cannot make this shit up," Nikolai muttered, pale-faced.

Mae spotted rail tracks in the distance. She scanned the road ahead, her heart racing. They were two hundred feet from the state police helicopter.

"Turn!"

Vlad glanced at her. "What?!"

"Turn! *Now!*"

Mae grabbed the steering wheel and yanked it to the right. Magic warmed her flesh as she unleashed *Wind Fury*.

The spell froze the traffic that would have crashed into them as they careened through an intersection and hurtled across the opposite highway. Mae's fingers almost dented the dashboard when the Bentley's side mirror missed a bus by mere inches.

They shot onto a side road. Mae ended the spell.

Metal groaned and crunched behind them. One of the patrol cars had smashed into the front end of a moving truck. Another skidded and crashed sideways into a traffic-light post to avoid the bus.

Mae looked away from the mayhem they'd left behind and studied the way ahead with a scowl. "Take a left!"

This time, Vlad obeyed her without question.

The Bentley's tires lifted off the road briefly as it swerved onto a street that ran behind a gas station and an automobile repair shop. A chain link-fence gate appeared at the end. Vlad gripped the steering wheel and floored the gas.

The Bentley smashed through the gate and bolted into a construction site.

"Head for the tracks!" Mae said urgently, glancing over her shoulder. "They should slow down the patrol cars!"

"They'll slow down the Bentley too," Vlad protested.

"I'll conjure a weak version of Wind Fury under your car."

Vlad narrowed his eyes at her. "Have you done this before, princess?"

Mae grimaced. "No."

Nikolai pressed a hand against the roof as Vlad maneuvered the Bentley up a dirt road that led to the railway line. He drove onto the tracks and pointed the car south, stone chipping rattling against the undercarriage.

Magic thrummed across Mae's bond with Brimstone and Hellreaver. She concentrated on creating a controlled version of *Wind Fury* underneath the car. Invisible currents whooshed into life with a low roar.

Vlad's eyes widened as the Bentley's ride went from bumpy to smooth. "Whoa!"

Nikolai stared out at the railway line. "Can't you just fly us out of here?"

Vlad grunted. "That's the first good idea this guy's had all day."

Mae clenched her teeth. "That's not how this works. If I put more power into this spell, it'll either rip the car apart or send it hurtling into the sky."

They both sobered at that.

The sound of rotors rose behind them. Gunfire peppered the tracks. Debris and rocks clouded the air.

The gunship was on their tail, the state police helicopter trailing in its wake.

Mae narrowed her eyes. *It's not going to be easy to lose these guys!*

She took a deep breath, maintained control of *Wind Fury*, and cast *Nullify*. To her chagrin, the spell confirmed the absence of black magic among the men in the aircrafts. None of them was a sorcerer. Which meant she couldn't go around getting rid of them willy-nilly.

A pair of factories appeared on their right. The railway line continued past them onto a bridge up ahead.

She was pondering whether *Ice Fortress* could freeze the helicopters' fuel lines when a massive explosion rocked the oil depot they were passing.

Mae's heart stuttered. Time slowed.

Brimstone's snarl sounded dimly in her ears. Hellreaver dropped from her neck and transformed, demonic energy flaring around his blades. Their magic augmented her own as she unleashed the only spell that could protect them.

"ECLIPSE!"

A black hole exploded in the sky.

Crimson enveloped Vlad and Tarang as they prepared to counter the effects of the detonation.

Whiteness filled Nikolai's eyes. He pressed his hands to the window. Alastair's pupils blazed as he gripped his sorcerer's shoulder.

"*Moon Shield!*" the sorcerer roared.

Eclipse sucked the flames and oxygen out of the giant fireball racing toward them and the work plants. The barrier Nikolai erected protected the Bentley and the hangars from the brunt of the shockwave that accompanied the explosion.

The car juddered on its suspension as the aftershock washed over them in a gust of dark smoke.

"These assholes really are trying to kill us, aren't they?!" Vlad ground out.

Mae glared at the gunship. Firing a grenade at the depot to try and stop them had been beyond reckless. Had the explosion reached the factories, there would undoubtedly have been civilian casualties.

To her surprise, the state police helicopter shot ahead of the military aircraft and swerved around to block its path. She clenched her teeth. It didn't matter that Jared was trying to prevent the gunship from blowing them to smithereens. She needed to stop them.

Mae closed her eyes and sought out an ice spell that could immobilize the aircrafts without killing anyone inside. One came to her slowly, the runes making up the conjuration rising languidly from the depths of her consciousness.

She opened her eyes. *I hope this works!*

Mae focused her magic, put the window down, and raised a hand toward the helicopters. "*Ice Storm!*"

Clouds darkened the sky. A blizzard exploded into existence around the two helicopters. They rolled and yawed, engines whining as their fuel lines started to freeze.

The spell kept them afloat within a violent squall of snow and ice.

Mae settled back into her seat and closed the window. "Go!"

Vlad floored the gas.

Wind Fury got the Bentley across the bridge without further incident. A wetland appeared on the other side of the river. Mae's heart sank.

Patrol cars had blocked off the tracks.

Her scalp prickled as bursts of magic that were not her own resonated with her core. Nikolai swore.

Vlad slammed on the brakes. "Son of a—!"

A veritable barrage of spell bombs had bloomed into life ahead of the patrol cars. It was an army of sorcerers and witches headed by Bryony and Abraham.

CHAPTER TWENTY

THE SOUNDPROOF ROOM DEEP BENEATH THE U.S. ARMY facility on Staten Island possessed all the charm of a death row chamber in a maximum-security prison.

Mae wrinkled her nose. *I can't believe Nikolai spent days exorcising people down here.*

The shackles securing her wrist and ankle cuffs to the floor jingled faintly as she shifted in the metal chair she'd been sitting in for going on two hours. The chains hummed as magic seeped into them from the jade and golden circles surrounding her.

Bryony and Abraham's binding spells would have stung her flesh were it not for *Soul Shield*.

Another fifteen minutes passed.

Mae frowned at the cameras dotting the corners of the ceiling. *I wonder how long they're going to leave me stewing here.*

A thread of disquiet danced through her. She'd been separated from Brimstone and Hellreaver when they'd been apprehended outside Boston. Though the fox and the demonic weapon had wanted to obliterate the enemy who had captured them off the surface of the Earth in their rage, Mae had insisted they keep their calm. She couldn't hurt their former allies, however much they currently loathed her very existence.

Besides, being here might give us a clue as to how to find that woman.

The despair and fear she'd read in the eyes of the witch the Dark Council were using to fight an invisible war against her reminded Mae all too much of what she'd glimpsed in Nikolai's gaze last night.

It was hard to see a way out of this when the entire world seemed to be against them.

She could sense the sorcerer and Vlad in the upper levels of the facility. They were unharmed, for now. Unbeknownst to their captors, she'd activated *Soul Shield* around everyone's cores the moment they'd stepped out of Vlad's Bentley, back at the rail tracks. And that included their familiars.

Brimstone and Hellreaver were being held behind several layers of heavy security in a sub-basement three floors beneath her. They were in separate cells and their anger at being forcibly parted from her still simmered across their bond with her.

A familiar magic flitted across her skin.

Mae took a shallow breath. *Here we go.*

The doors to the chamber opened. Abraham walked in, his owl Shiloh on his shoulder and Jared at his side.

Mae narrowed her eyes as they crossed the floor.

"Took you long enough. As far as I remember, I didn't waive my right to an attorney."

Jared studied her coldly from where he'd stopped outside the magic circles. "You waived that right when you killed all those people."

Mae decided against protesting her innocence and telling them the violent acts they'd witnessed in those video clips were all in their heads. It'd been crystal clear since the day before that one of the mirage magic's intentions was to make her allies loathe her just for being alive.

Her gaze shifted to Abraham. "It seems magic is open knowledge in this illusion. This will make things easier. Release me before I bring this entire facility down on your heads."

Abraham's eyes flashed gold. The runes around her brightened.

Mae clenched her jaw when the sorcerer's power licked at *Soul Shield*.

It stank of the mirage magic afflicting him.

"You speak as if this is all some kind of game!" Abraham spat out. "You should be begging me not to kill you, Witch Queen!"

Mae grimaced. "Wow. This spell sure did a number on you."

Abraham glared at her. "Your lies mean nothing to me. You're a monster and you'll be treated as such."

Mae swallowed a sigh. There was no point getting frustrated. Trying to convince them that what they were feeling toward her was the true lie when they were still under the effect of the mirage magic was going to be as effective as talking to a brick wall. She turned her attention to Jared.

"You should have spent more time with your friends in Chicago, like Violet and Miles. If you had, you would have been protected by their divine power and I wouldn't have to kick your ass on the way out of here."

The Immortal recoiled. He recovered and took a threatening step toward her.

"What do you know about Chicago?!"

"It's the place where you got that divine sword you wield." Mae's gaze dropped briefly to the hidden switchblade strapped to his left ankle. "The one the guy who's going to be my ally made for you."

Jared lowered his brows, a muscle twitching in his cheek. "I don't know how you got that information, but I doubt Artemus would ever mingle with the likes of you. As for Violet and Miles Nolan, we'll soon free them from your wicked enchantment."

Mae leaned back in the chair, a mocking half-smile playing on her lips. "Not if they beat you first. FYI, Artemus will probably do the same when this is over."

Jared's expression turned ugly. "Why you—!"

"Don't!" Abraham warned as the Immortal rushed toward her.

Jared stepped inside the magic circles.

Heat filled Mae's belly.

The runes around her shifted from green and gold to a violent red.

"Contain!"

A crimson bubble burst around Jared. The Immortal cursed as he found himself trapped inside her prison. He removed the knife from his ankle and unleashed the holy sword within.

"This is gonna hurt." Mae narrowed her eyes. *"Sever!"*

The spell engulfed Jared. He groaned, dropped the blade, and doubled over, teeth bared in a grimace of pure agony and knuckles white where he gripped his skull.

Abraham cursed. *"Shield!"*

His spell bounced off *Contain.*

Mae shifted forward in the chair and focused her powers past Jared's pain to the thread that would unravel the mirage magic that had obscured his true memories. The sword drew her eye where it lay on the floor. She frowned, an idea coming to her.

Assimilate!

The blade trembled, the power it contained resisting her attempts to consume it. Jared fell to his knees.

Mae ground her teeth. *Absorb!*

Golden light bloomed on the surface of the sword. It faded a moment later.

Mae concentrated on Jared's consciousness once more. The doors opened just as she found what she was looking for.

Bryony and Valentina Flores barged inside the chamber.

"*Shield!*" the two witches barked.

Mae felt their protection spark around Jared. The Immortal's eyes rolled into the back of his head. He collapsed on the floor. She shuddered and withdrew her magic, her heart thundering against her ribs. The runes surrounding her regained their original colors.

Did it work?!

Hate burned in Abraham's eyes as he dragged Jared out of the circles.

Bryony glanced at Valentina, her expression cold. "Do it."

Indigo shackles exploded around Mae. She gasped as they wrapped around her forehead, body, and limbs, pinning her to the chair. Her gaze found the witch who'd attacked her, the insidious magic in the new chains licking at *Soul Shield.*

"What the hell is this?!"

A look of distaste twisted Valentina's face. She stepped inside the magic circles. "Something I am loath to do since it involves touching you, but I cannot ignore the command of my superior."

Mae blinked. *Her sup—?!*

The corruption that descended around her snatched the rest of her words from her lips. Mae grunted as an agonizing pressure weighed her down. Concrete cracked beneath her feet. The chair groaned as it sank a couple of inches into the ground.

Barquiel's power burned Mae's throat and made her flesh itch.

To her utter lack of surprise, Bryony, Abraham, and

Valentina seemed unaffected by the demon archduke's energy.

Mae's gaze swept the chamber for her enemy while Valentina pressed her fingers against her temples. It took but seconds to find the blonde figure framed in the doorway.

Rose smiled beatifically. "Hello, Mae."

CHAPTER TWENTY-ONE

Mae clenched her jaw until her teeth ached. "When it rains, it fucking pours, huh? How about you come over here so I can punch your pretty face?!"

She noted Bryony and Abraham bowing deferentially as Rose strolled inside the chamber at a leisurely pace.

The demon put her hands on her hips and tilted her head to the side. "My, my, you sure are full of vim and vigor today. I'm afraid that's gonna be impossible real soon."

Mae stiffened. "What do you mean—?"

"*Seal,*" Valentina said grimly.

Icy fire exploded inside Mae's head. She choked, her vision blurring and the taste of blood blooming on her tongue.

What—is this?!

She was vaguely conscious of Rose approaching as she drew on *Soul Shield*. A vile stench flooded her nostrils when the demon leaned down and brought her lips to her ear.

"Why, this is just a spell that will lock your magic and that endless grimoire inside your head." Rose straightened a little and stared at Mae, her face inches from hers. Glee brightened her gray eyes, the pupils in the center crimson pools of triumph and hate. "Once it's done, I will carve out your brain and take it back to the Dark Council. Vedran and Dietrich will spend weeks examining every inch of your dead flesh." A crazed chuckle left her throat. "Why, I might even toss your remains in Hell so your poor father can find you and grieve your second passing."

Her words etched themselves in Mae's mind in violent shades of red. Mae grimaced and arched as Valentina's spell scraped her consciousness, the pain so fierce she was surprised she hadn't screamed yet. She blinked and panted. "Bar…quiel?!"

Rose leaned in, curiosity mixing with loathing. "Yes?"

Mae swallowed convulsively and moved even closer. "I'm going to cut your vile heart out of your chest and hand it to you before this war is over!"

The conjuration she'd been working on since she entered the facility solidified inside her core, the divine energy she'd absorbed from Jared's weapon the last piece she'd needed to complete it.

"SUMMON!" Mae growled.

Crimson detonated around her. Valentina cried out, the silent explosion of power lifting her off her feet and sending her flying across the magic circles and into Bryony and Abraham.

Barquiel jumped back and shifted into his true form.

The air inside the chamber trembled. Hellreaver whooshed into view and blocked the demon's claws as they sailed toward Mae's heart, an unholy sound of rage erupting from his jagged blades.

Brimstone materialized in his full guise, his eyes glowing with fury and his vibrating tails sending plaster dust raining around them. He sank his teeth into Barquiel's wing and cast him violently aside.

Bryony and Abraham stared in horror at the demon where he'd smashed into a wall. Brimstone's shadow fell upon them. They leaned back in alarm when the fox lowered his massive head toward them.

"I do not care that you were once our friends!" he growled, flecks of drool dripping from his jaws and splashing at their feet. *"If you ever hurt my witch again, I will end you myself!"*

The New York coven witch and sorcerer blanched. Penley and Shiloh trembled next to them.

A burst of powerful black magic fluttered across Mae's skin.

Dread twisted her stomach.

It was coming from where Nikolai was.

She destroyed the fetters binding her to the floor and rose inside a red sphere of power, Brimstone and Hellreaver at her side.

❄

"Where's Alastair?" Nikolai asked coldly.

"Your familiar is safe, my liege," one of the New York coven members guarding him replied awkwardly. "He's in a room at the end of the corridor." His troubled gaze darted to Vlad. "Along with the, er, tiger."

The incubus observed the sorcerer who'd spoken with narrowed eyes from where he sat at the opposite end of the conference table from Nikolai. Neither of them had been cuffed after being detained outside Boston. The only one who'd been treated like a criminal had been Mae, the disgust and hatred directed at her almost palpable as she was bundled into the back of an armored van with a bunch of sorcerers and witches. Though they hadn't seen her since being brought to the facility, they knew she was close.

Soul Shield was active inside both of them, its power warming their bodies.

Nikolai studied the witches and sorcerers guarding the exits. It was clear from the glances they cast his way when they thought he wasn't looking that they held him in high regard, even though they believed he was not in his right mind right now. He wondered if they would remember their misbegotten actions when the mirage magic lifted.

From what Cortes had described and Mrs. Son-Ha had inferred, it seemed the spell eventually faded after the person who unleashed it achieved their goals. In the case of the Dark Council, that would be after they'd chained him to their side and killed Mae.

Bitterness churned Nikolai's stomach.

Even if my father and Barquiel's scheme doesn't succeed,

the New York coven may never recover from this. Betraying Mae is something they won't easily forgive themselves for.

"Just so you know, Tarang needs three set meals a day," Vlad told their guards. "I wouldn't want one of your friends to become an accidental snack, so you better make sure you feed him on time. He likes steak."

The sorcerers and witches frowned at the incubus.

Nikolai suspected the only reason Vlad wasn't chained up in a cell right now was because the *Black Devils* still carried influence in their altered memories.

One of the witches mistook his expression.

"Do not worry, my liege," she reassured him. "You will soon be freed from that wicked woman's spell."

Tension knotted Nikolai's shoulders. *What are they planning?*

He shared a guarded glance with Vlad before addressing the witch. "And how do you intend to do that, exactly?" His tone turned grim. "Do you guys have another of those altars in the basement?"

Confusion clouded the witch's eyes. She shared an uncertain glance with her companions.

Nikolai clenched his jaw. *It seems they know nothing of the altar that triggered the mirage spell.*

Vlad rose, demonic energy flashing in his pupils and upon his flesh. He lowered his brows and glared at something beyond Nikolai's shoulder.

There was a sound behind Nikolai. The voice that spoke next sent a chill down his spine and had him bolting to his feet. He whirled around and sent the chair clattering to the ground.

"There is no need for an altar, brother," Oscar said

with a smile that didn't reach his eyes as he stepped out of a rift with his lynx Drabek.

The hairs rose on Nikolai's arms. It was one of Barquiel's portals.

Shit. He must be here too!

He sensed the demon's energy a heartbeat later. It was coming from somewhere below them.

Vlad startled and looked at the floor before meeting Nikolai's alarmed gaze. "Fuck!"

Fear twisted Nikolai's insides. *Mae!*

Corruption pulsed from Oscar. Drabek's eyes darkened to obsidian.

"*Contain*," the sorcerer said with a lazy flick of a hand.

Oily tendrils of darkness filled the room. They converged and formed cages around Nikolai and Vlad before either of them could move. The incubus cursed and smashed the translucent barrier with a fist, to no avail. Nikolai heard Tarang's distant roar above the sound of blood pounding in his skull.

His gaze was locked on the dark sphere forming above Oscar's left hand. It reeked of the magic Mae had unleashed inside the church.

How is he doing that?!

Something glittered inside the inky globe. It took a moment to make out a stone covered in blazing, blue runes spinning inside the orb.

CHAPTER TWENTY-TWO

Oscar sneered. "Don't worry, I hear it only hurts for a minute."

Nikolai scowled. "What are you going to do with that?!"

Oscar shrugged, amusement replacing the disdain on his face. "Why, I'm going to bury it deep inside you, brother. So deep your sweet Mae won't ever find it."

Ice filled Nikolai's veins as he looked from Oscar's scornful expression to the stone. He finally recognized his father's intentions.

The surest way to bring him back to the Dark Council was to make him forget about Mae.

Nikolai's body heated up as he drew on his magic, his bond with Alastair strong and true despite the distance between them. The air inside the translucent cage surrounding him shimmered with the pale light of his Moon Magic and white magic. He raised a hand.

"*Moon Spear!*"

A dazzling bolt erupted from his palm and smashed into Oscar's shield. A crack appeared.

Oscar lowered his brows. His eyes darkened a second before black magic detonated around him.

"ROT!"

Nikolai's ears popped. He grunted, legs caving slightly as the pressure of Oscar's spell weighed him down. A violent, scarlet aura made the air tremble around Vlad as he resisted the corrupt magic attempting to bring him to his knees.

Choked-off screams rent the air. The New York coven witches and sorcerers fell to the ground and started convulsing.

Oscar didn't even spare them a glance.

Nikolai's stomach curdled as he watched the thrashing figures' foaming mouths and jerking bodies. He knew instinctively that the only reason he and Vlad weren't going through the exact same thing right now was because of Mae's *Soul Shield*.

"Is that your father's magic I can feel mixed in with his?" Vlad said between clenched teeth. "This spell is way stronger than anything this asshole has shown us before!"

Nikolai had to concur. There was a sinister echo to Oscar's spell. One his brother had not possessed before.

"He's right." A nasty expression twisted Oscar's features as he looked from Vlad to Nikolai. "Father decided to lend me some of his strength to accomplish this most hallowed task." His eyes shrank to slits. "However much I may loathe your return, there is no doubt you are essential to our schemes. Besides, father is very keen to study your new powers, *brother*."

Revulsion tightened Nikolai's throat. He could only imagine what that would entail.

Oscar smiled coldly. "*Disperse*."

Nikolai gasped. He could feel his magic being drained.

He barely had time to draw on his core before Oscar stepped up to him, reached through *Contain*, and punched the dark orb in his hand inside his belly.

"Nikolai!" Vlad barked.

Nikolai's breath froze. His eyes rounded as he stared from where Oscar's hand had entered his body to his brother's triumphant face.

Oscar's gleeful smile slowly faded at Nikolai's lack of reaction. "What the hell is that?"

Nikolai swallowed. *He must mean* Soul Shield!

Oscar's lip curled. "It seems that bitch is still trying to protect you even though Barquiel is torturing her right now." He smirked. "How cute. Don't worry, it won't be long before we bring you her corpse."

The aura around Vlad thickened with rage. "You bastards won't get away with this!"

Wrath ignited Nikolai's core. He scowled and grabbed Oscar's wrist.

"*Hell Flare!*"

Black and crimson flames exploded into life and raced up Oscar's arm. He cursed and withdrew his hand from Nikolai's body before batting at the magic fire, the dark orb in his grasp fading with a hiss of corruption. Drabek backpedaled at his side, eyes full of loathing. Having experienced *Hell Flare* once before in Prague, it looked like neither the sorcerer nor his lynx familiar were keen for a repeat.

The building trembled. Oscar startled and stumbled.

Nikolai almost lost his balance as the floor shook violently beneath his feet. A familiar power brushed against his consciousness. His pulse quickened.

Mae!

The ground exploded upward. A violent outburst of crimson magic flooded the room and smashed all the windows.

Mae rose through the gaping hole alongside Brimstone and Hellreaver. Her furious gaze found Nikolai and Vlad.

"Are you guys okay?!"

Relief brightened Vlad's eyes. "Never better, princess. We sure as hell are glad to see you!"

Mae clenched her jaw. "Hell, go free Alastair and Tarang!"

Hellreaver flashed across the chamber and smashed through a wall. The sound of exploding concrete trailed in his wake as he carved a path through the building.

Brimstone bared his fangs at Oscar. *"It looks like there's a rat in the building, my witch!"*

Oscar glowered at them as he backed away, Drabek hissing around his ankles.

Mae narrowed her eyes at the Sorcerer King's heir. A wall of scarlet spell bombs bloomed in front of her.

Oscar swore when he grasped her intent. *"Shie—!"*

His incantation ended on a grunt as she blasted him and his familiar straight through a wall and out of the complex.

They dropped from view, their angry voices fading.

Mae landed lightly in front of Nikolai and Vlad. "We should—!"

The air trembled violently. Mae whirled around.

Barquiel's power choked Nikolai's throat in the next instant. Vlad cursed.

A feral sound left Brimstone's chest as the demon who had killed Na Ri ascended through the opening in the floor. Mae unleashed *Devour* and *Eclipse,* her pupils glowing with an incandescent light.

The air ripped open between them and the demon before they could charge at one another.

Alicia stepped out of a rift in her Soul Reaper form, her raven cloak fluttering in an invisible wind and her dark scythe gleaming with a trace of the cold, red light radiating out of her orbits. She looked around, scowled when she saw Barquiel, and leveled a narrow-eyed stare at Mae.

"I was only gone for a day. What the hell happened?!"

Mae swallowed. "You—you remember who I am?!"

"Of course I remember who you are," Alicia snapped. She stilled. "Wait. Does that mean—?"

The roar that drowned out the Reaper's words rattled the building and made plaster dust quake down from the ceiling.

"*HOW DARE YOU INSECTS FORGET MY*

PRESENCE?!" Barquiel shrieked, spit flying from his jaws.

Alicia's expression grew pinched. "This guy is such a diva."

Mae's pupils flared. *"Negate!"*

Goosebumps raced across Nikolai's skin as her spell started to consume the storm of demonic power and black magic swirling around the howling fiend. His core throbbed a second before Alastair flew inside the room ahead of Tarang and Hellreaver.

The crow landed on Nikolai's shoulder and butted his cheek lovingly with his head. Relief lightened Nikolai's chest as he stroked his familiar. His shoulders knotted as he looked around.

Cracks were appearing in the walls.

"We should get out of here before he brings the place down on our heads!"

Alicia and Mae regrouped with him and Vlad.

"They'll be right on our tail again if we leave here the normal way!" Mae told Nikolai. "How about you use *Transmigrate?!*"

Nikolai startled. "What?!"

Mae made a face. "I know you've been practicing that spell."

"The crow told me," Brimstone explained at Nikolai's shocked stare.

Alastair carefully avoided Nikolai's narrow-eyed gaze.

"What's the problem?" Vlad snapped. "You shy? You want us to turn around so you can slip that spell out of your garter or something?"

Nikolai clenched his jaw. "You fucker!" He dropped to one knee and pressed a hand to the floor. "I hope you barf on the way to the nexus!"

"He's so easy to get a reaction out of," Vlad remarked to Mae. "You should train him better."

Mae rolled her eyes. Alicia sighed.

Bryony and Abraham stumbled into view through what remained of the doorway moments after Nikolai found the ley line beneath the facility. Their eyes bulged as they stared at Barquiel.

Bryony reached out a hand to Nikolai. "My liege, please!"

Nikolai ground his teeth and focused on the magic blazing through his and Alastair's cores. "Get ready!"

"How about I find you guys later?" Alicia shifted into her human form, her expression that of someone who'd just realized something unpleasant. "I don't think I should go to the—"

"TRANSMIGRATE!"

CHAPTER TWENTY-THREE

"UGH," ALICIA GROANED.

Mae grimaced. "Was it really that bad?"

"It was worse than bad." The Reaper Queen slumped in the chair and rubbed her temples. "Is this what you people call a migraine?"

"Probably," Nikolai said guiltily.

They were back at Mrs. Son-Ha's place.

To Mae's surprise, the nexus under New York had been even bigger than the one under Prague.

"That's because there's more people in this city," Nikolai had explained while she and Vlad stared at the enormous rivers of magic pouring into the dazzling space around them.

Like the one in Prague, it seemed to have no boundaries.

Mae had not heard Ran Soyun's voice this time around.

Nikolai and Alastair had replenished their cores with white magic before reversing *Transmigrate* and bringing them out in Mrs. Son-Ha's backyard. To Mae's utter lack of surprise, the old woman had been waiting for them like a grim sentinel.

"What took you guys so long?" she'd grumbled as she'd put down her knitting needles. "The tea's cold."

A chorus of excited yips preceded Vlad as he wandered inside the kitchen presently. Mrs. Son-Ha's dogs jumped excitedly around his legs while he frowned at his phone. "I can't get through to Cortes."

"I'd know if he was in trouble. I cast *Soul Shield* around him and Popo before they left this morning." Mae's curious gaze dropped to the bouncing dogs. "Do you have treats in your pockets or does your incubus power work on animals too?"

"What a suggestive question, princess." Vlad's mouth stretched in a smile that made Mae's cheeks heat up. He ignored Nikolai's darkening expression and arched an eyebrow at Mae. "Who knows. Shall we try a human experiment and see?"

Mae bit her lip. Even the way the incubus arched his eyebrow was sinfully sexy.

"Seriously wishing you guys would stop flirting right now," Alicia grumbled. "Your voices are echoing inside my skull."

She winced when Vlad pulled out a chair.

"What's the matter with her?" the incubus asked.

"She has a headache."

"Ah." Vlad grimaced. "I have to admit, being exposed to such a vast amount of white magic wasn't exactly pleasant. It must have been doubly worse for her, considering what she is."

"Thanks," Alicia muttered.

"Shame you didn't barf," Nikolai told the incubus nastily.

Alicia's skin took on a greenish tinge. "How about no one mention bodily functions for a while? I'm barely hanging on to breakfast as it is."

Mrs. Son-Ha put a pot of tea on the table and squinted at Alicia. "Are you guys sure this woman is the Queen of Soul Reapers? She looks kinda feeble."

Alicia opened an eye and studied their host. "I've been meaning to ask. Who is this? And why do I smell the presence of so many soul remnants in her house?"

Mrs. Son-Ha sniffed and crossed her arms. "I'm a Shaman."

Alicia blinked and straightened. "Get out of here!"

Mrs. Son-Ha scowled. "It's my place, lady."

"That's not what I me—oh, never mind." Alicia sighed. "Just so you know, there are only a handful of real Shamans in the world. The rest are charlatans." She lowered her brows, her tone turning suspicious. "One thing I *am* certain of. Shamans do not possess the ability to erect divine barriers."

Mrs. Son-Ha shrugged. "That's not me."

They told Alicia about Camael and the dragon bell.

"Oh God." The Reaper Queen's expression turned glassy as she stared at the artifact sitting innocuously on the windowsill. "Astarte will have a coronary when I tell her about this." She pinched the bridge of her nose. "I bet Armaros just laughs his damn head off."

Mae blinked. "Armaros?"

"He's part of Astarte's alliance," Alicia explained.

"He's a fallen angel and the eleventh leader of the Grigori. His name was the Accursed One and he was Heaven's most talented blacksmith before he was banished to the Underworld."

Mae startled.

Hellreaver quivered on her chest. *Ar—Armaros!*

Brimstone blinked his eyes open and raised his head where he'd been snoozing by the back door with Tarang. *Ah.*

Mae looked warily from the weapon to the fox. "What is it?"

I do believe that's the name of Hellreaver's maker.

Hellreaver practically vibrated off Mae's chest. *He's right, my witch!*

Her eyes rounded. "Really? Then—can he fix the skeleton key?!"

"What are you talking about?" Nikolai said, puzzled.

"Armaros is the one who made Hellreaver," Mae explained excitedly.

Alicia stared. "Oh." She slammed her fist into her palm. "That makes total sense!"

"Is that skeleton key even relevant anymore?" Vlad asked Mae dubiously. "Since it appears the Dark Council already has their hands on the *Book of Shadows*, I can't see the urgency in getting it fixed."

"I—"

Mae faltered. What the incubus had said was technically correct. Still, she couldn't help but feel that key was important.

Call it a witch's instincts.

"Something tells me we might need it one day."

I agree, my witch, Brimstone murmured.

A sliver of unease flitted through Mae. The fox had been strangely out of sorts since they'd returned from the nexus. She was about to ask him what was troubling him when a hum distracted her.

The dragon bell was quivering on the windowsill.

Mrs. Son-Ha frowned. "Someone just crossed the barrier around the house."

Vlad rose, demonic energy flaring in his pupils.

The old woman waved a dismissive hand at him. "How about you put away the creepy glowing eyes? It's unlikely to be an enemy. The barrier wouldn't have let them through."

Mae recognized the cores of the pair climbing the steps to the porch. She tensed when she detected a different energy behind them. "Oh."

"What?" Nikolai said guardedly.

The doorbell rang. Mrs. Son-Ha shuffled out of the kitchen and returned a moment later with Violet and Miles.

Jared entered the room behind them.

Brimstone growled and straightened off the floor. Nikolai stood up and joined Vlad as the incubus stepped protectively in front of Mae. Alicia narrowed her eyes at the Immortal.

Mae had told them what had happened in the basement at the army facility on Staten Island.

Violet and Miles blinked when they registered the battery of hostile stares being aimed at Jared.

"What's the matter?" Violet asked, confused.

Trixie rubbed her nose uneasily with her paws where she perched on the witch's shoulder.

Jared's expression turned awkward as he met Mae's gaze. He scratched the back of his head. "Hey."

Mae relaxed. She couldn't feel the wrongness she'd detected inside him back on Staten Island.

"Looks like you're back to your normal self," she told the Immortal.

Nikolai jerked around. "You broke the mirage spell he was under?!"

"What?!" Violet lowered her brows accusingly at Jared. "You were influenced by the spell too?"

"But—how come?" Miles blurted out. "We presumed you wouldn't be!"

A heavy sigh left Jared. "Look, it's not as if I could help it, okay?"

"The two of you have spent more time with your friends in Chicago than he has," Mae told Violet and Miles. "It's the divine power you've absorbed from them that protected you from losing your memories."

Violet and Miles exchanged a stunned look.

"How did you get rid of the mirage magic affecting Jared?" Violet mumbled.

"*Sever* worked on him." Mae forestalled the question bubbling on the witch's lips with a grimace. "But only because he's an Immortal. It wouldn't work on anyone else."

Violet visibly drooped.

"How did you two even meet?" A suspicious frown wrinkled Miles's brow as he looked from Jared to Mae. "Wait. Did something happen? There was a lot of activity at the Boston coven just before we left the place."

Mae made a face. "It's a long story."

Nikolai and Vlad helped Mrs. Son-Ha prepare dinner while Mae brought Violet and Miles up to speed on what had happened when they'd visited Marblehead Neck and their subsequent arrest.

Jared grew pale the more he listened. "Shit. I turned a gunship on you?!"

"To be fair, you did try to stop it." Mae watched him closely. "You don't remember any of it?"

"It all feels like a really weird dream." A muscle jumped in his jawline. "Or a nightmare, even." The Immortal faltered. "All I remember is a lingering feeling of hate toward you."

Mae exchanged a careful look with Nikolai. Their suspicions regarding the other effect of the mirage magic had just been proven to be correct.

"How did you know you'd find us here?" Vlad asked the Immortal.

"I didn't." Jared grimaced. "I called Violet once I woke up and got out of that place. FYI, the facility was a mess when I left it."

Guilt stabbed through Mae. "Did Bryony and Abraham get hurt?"

Jared shook his head. "No. And there were no fatalities, luckily." He frowned at her. "By the way, did you do something to my sword?" He removed the switchblade from his ankle and studied it warily. "It feels different."

"Oh, that?" Mae wrinkled her nose. "I, er, absorbed

its power."

Jared blinked.

Alicia's eyes bulged. "You did what?!"

Mae squirmed under their shocked stares.

"I needed something extra to make a new spell," she said defensively. "Since Jared didn't have any divine energy in his soul I could assimilate, I took it from his sword instead."

The Immortal looked a little bit sick at that.

"It wasn't going to kill you," she mumbled.

"The stuff you do scares me sometimes, princess," Vlad said soberly.

Nikolai looked similarly grave where he stood with a knife and carrot held aloft.

Violet and Miles shared an excited glance. "Wait till we tell Artemus and the others about this!"

Mae wasn't sure she liked the sound of that.

"The barrier around this place should replenish your sword's energy," she reassured a worried Jared.

The Immortal's shoulders unknotted. He sat next to Alicia and observed her waxen complexion curiously. "What's the matter with her?"

CHAPTER TWENTY-FOUR

remembered what he'd snatched from Oscar during
their fight at the facility on Staten Island.

"I'd totally forgotten about this."

He removed the black stone that had been inside
the mirage magic orb Oscar had manifested from his
jacket and put it on the table.

The others stared at it. It was perfectly smooth, like
a pebble.

"Oscar tried to use this on me," Nikolai explained.

Mae stiffened at his words.

"You mean, when he put that orb inside you?" Vlad
said suspiciously.

"Yes." Nikolai met Mae's troubled gaze. "It was
covered in runes made of the same blue fire we saw on
the altar in that church."

Mae picked up the stone. She frowned.

Though the flames had gone out, there was the

barest hint of scorch marks where the symbols had once been.

Crimson flared in her pupils.

Nikolai drew a sharp breath as scarlet lines exploded across the item, mapping out the runes that had been there.

"Whoa," Violet mumbled.

Mrs. Son-Ha sipped her tea and watched avidly.

Hope sent Nikolai's heart racing. "Can you trace the altar and the woman you saw in your vision using this stone?"

Mae hesitated. "I doubt it, but I'll try."

Everyone watched breathlessly as she closed her hand around the object and focused. Redness bloomed around her. The plates on the table vibrated.

Her magic warmed his skin as it washed over him. *"Reveal."*

Tension knotted Nikolai's stomach.

Mae wrinkled her brow. "Like I thought, it's not enough on its own." Her mouth pressed into a thin line. "And I can't decipher this magic either."

Nikolai's shoulders slumped.

The dragon bell hummed.

Mrs. Son-Ha started to rise. "Who is it now?"

Everyone tensed when the front door of the house opened. The dogs yipped excitedly and bolted out into the hallway. Their host narrowed her eyes. Cortes entered the kitchen with a drooping Popo.

"Did you just use your magic on my front door?"

"Yes," Cortes said shamelessly.

Mrs. Son-Ha grumbled something under her breath. She headed for the stove. "You had dinner yet?"

"I'm not hungry." Cortes noticed Jared and Alicia's presence as he pulled out a chair. "What are they doing here?"

"Alicia came to our rescue after Jared and the New York coven arrested us," Mae explained.

Cortes stilled.

Jared sighed at his deathly glare. "Mae broke the spell I was under."

Cortes arched an eyebrow at Mae. "You broke the mirage magic?"

He jumped a little when Mrs. Son-Ha put a loaded plate in front of him.

"Here, eat."

"I said I wasn't hun—"

The rest of his words were muffled by Mrs. Son-Ha shoving a forkful of beef stew and rice in his mouth.

"I won't have it said that I let my guests starve," the old woman said sharply.

Vlad smirked.

Cortes cut his eyes to the incubus, chewed, and slowly swallowed. "Are there carrots in this?"

The corners of Mrs. Son-Ha's eyes tightened. "Why, you got a problem with carrots?"

"No," Cortes denied.

He waited until she'd turned her back before stabbing a piece of the offensive vegetable with his fork and passing it to Popo. The parrot brightened up.

"Why does Popo look down?" Mae asked.

Cortes passed another carrot to the bird. "The meeting with my coven was…tense."

"Picky eaters have short lives, you know," Alicia drawled as he fed a third piece to his familiar.

The Columbian ignored the Reaper Queen. He appraised Mae, Nikolai, and Vlad with a narrow-eyed stare. "So, what happened to you?"

They got him up to speed while he ate.

Cortes's shoulders tensed when Mae mentioned Barquiel. "The demon turned up?"

He'd seen Barquiel for the first time in Prague.

"Yeah." Mae's expression grew pinched. "He made Valentina Flores use a spell to try and seal my powers. From what Barquiel revealed, it appears Vedran wants to get his hands on the magic treasure trove inside my head." She grimaced at Jared. "Oh, and he mentioned Dietrich."

The Immortal lowered his brows. Dietrich Farago was currently the Immortal Societies' number one most wanted person.

"My father also wants to make me forget about Mae," Nikolai said darkly. "Oscar intended to use mirage magic to get me to join their side."

Hope brightened Mae's eyes.

"What about you?" she asked Cortes. "Did your coven provide you with any names?"

A strange expression danced across Cortes's face. "They're working on it."

"What is it?" Mae said curiously.

Cortes shot a glance at Mrs. Son-Ha. "I…spoke to my family, like she suggested."

The old lady beamed.

"How'd it go?" Vlad asked warily.

Cortes studied his interlocked fingers.

"They confirmed what we spoke about," he said in a stilted voice. "That they were not in their right mind when Raya attacked me." Lines wrinkled his brow. "They said it felt like waking up from a horrible nightmare afterward."

"Yeah," Jared mumbled.

Mae chewed her lip. "Does that mean you'll reconcile with them?"

Cortes hesitated.

Vlad patted his shoulder. "Family is important in our world, Enrique. Why don't you kiss and make up?"

Cortes grunted. "Do you have to make everything sound dirty?"

Vlad grinned.

Nikolai studied Violet and Miles. "You didn't tell us what you found in Boston."

The cousins exchanged a troubled glance.

Violet scratched her cheek. "Not much, really. But we did confirm something."

Mae pursed her lips. "What?"

"We tracked down Leta Patton and asked her a couple of questions," Miles said.

Nikolai straightened.

Mae frowned. "Let me guess. She doesn't remember going to Marblehead Neck."

"Bingo," Violet mumbled.

Nikolai met Mae's troubled gaze. That came as no

surprise after everything they'd witnessed in the last thirty-six hours.

Mae turned to Alicia. "Is there a way you can locate the woman I saw in my vision?"

The Reaper Queen made a face. "That'd be like looking for a needle in the proverbial haystack. Even more so if Barquiel has one of his damn rifts surrounding that place."

Mae drooped.

Vlad's cell chimed. He took his phone out and frowned at the display before accepting the incoming call. "What is it?"

He stiffened and uncrossed his legs a couple of seconds later.

Nikolai's pulse quickened.

Vlad's eyes shrank to slits. "Where?"

It was close to midnight when they exited Interstate 95 and entered the outskirts of East Brunswick. Vlad's men were waiting for them in the parking lot of a Mormon church west of the town center.

Mae stepped out of the SUV the incubus had had the *Black Devils* deliver to them in Brooklyn. Though the chances of the Dark Council and the New York coven having infiltrated the Russian crime group were slim at best, there was no point taking any chances. Mrs. Son-Ha's place in Glendale needed to be kept out of sight of their enemies.

She looked around the deserted lot warily as Vlad's men headed over to them. Even though it was night time, she still felt exposed.

"Sorry boss, they gave us the slip after they left here," the man in the lead said briskly as he joined them. His eyes widened when he saw Mae. He rocked to a halt. "Er, isn't that—?"

"A woman you never saw," Vlad said coldly.

The man paled a little. He looked even more dumbfounded when Cortes stepped out of the SUV with Violet and Miles.

"What's going on, boss?" the second guy asked uneasily. "I mean, I know there's a truce in place and all, but aren't we technically at war with the *Bacatá Cartel?*"

Mae's mouth went dry.

Vlad froze. "Since when are we at war with the Columbians?"

The man in the lead exchanged an awkward glance with his companion. "Since that deal went south in that strip club on Broadway, three months ago. You know, when you and Vasco Gomez clashed. You killed him, remember?"

Nikolai lowered his brows.

Cortes's expression darkened. He met Vlad's perturbed gaze. "Looks like the story line in this illusion is meant to ensure we never become allies."

Mae fisted her hands. *He's right. Oscar and Vedran must have planned it this way deliberately.*

A muscle jumped in Vlad's jawline as he observed his men. "What's this truce you mentioned?"

The pair grew even more discomfited.

"Are you sure you're okay, boss?" The guy in the lead looked over at Mae. "She might be influencing—"

"This has nothing to do with her!" Vlad snapped.

The men flinched.

Vlad took a shaky breath, clearly annoyed with himself for having shouted at them.

Mae touched the incubus's arm and looked at his subordinates. "Just—answer his question, please."

"Our boss and theirs are intending to hold reconciliation talks next week," the second man explained reluctantly. He hesitated and shot a glance at Cortes. "Word is they may be trying to kill Yuliy."

Cortes ground his teeth. "We'd never do something that cowardly!"

"None of this is real," Mae warned. "So, how about everyone calm down?"

"Mae's right," Nikolai said while Vlad's men shared confused glances. "We need to focus on stopping the Dark Council, not a war that doesn't exist."

Vlad blew out a frustrated sigh and ran a hand through his hair. An anxious rumble escaped Tarang. The incubus ruffled the tiger's head before turning to stare at the church. "So, this is where you last saw Sergio Mendes and his people?"

"Yes," the man in the lead replied uneasily.

"Thanks, we'll take it from here."

They waited until the men left before finding a side door to the building.

Seeing as it was late on a Sunday night, the church was empty. They split up to explore the place.

"Why did Mendes come here?" Mae pondered.

Nikolai manifested a glowing orb of Moon Magic so they could examine the room they'd entered. The sorcerer shrugged. "Beats me. Maybe he came to confess his sins."

Mae pulled a face. "I really doubt that's the reason he and his coven visited this church."

They didn't uncover anything untoward in the rooms they checked out and soon joined Vlad and Cortes in the main prayer hall.

"You guys find anything?" Mae asked as they headed up the central aisle.

Vlad shuddered. "Apart from a reaffirmation of my loathing for all things religious, no."

Cortes blinked. "You don't have a faith?"

"Of course not." Vlad stared. "Do you?"

"Yeah, I do."

Vlad narrowed his eyes. "Is that pity I see on your face?"

"No." The Columbian sighed. "I'm just surprised, considering who you are. Your father is the King of Incubi and you people know archangels."

"Oh, I believe in Heaven and Hell," Vlad said with a dismissive wave of his hand. "I just choose not to pander to mankind's interpretation of it."

Violet's voice rose excitedly behind them. "Hey, we found something!"

Mae twisted around, her pulse quickening.

The witch came up the aisle with Miles. She was holding a black feather.

"You found a bird?" Vlad asked skeptically.

"No, just a bunch of these and some blood in the bishop's office at the back. It looked pretty fresh."

Mae's eyes widened. She could smell a taint of familiar magic coming off the feather.

Gold flashed in Cortes's eyes. He took the quill off Violet and carefully sniffed it. "This is from Mendes's harpy eagle."

"Take us to where you found that blood," Mae told Violet urgently.

CHAPTER TWENTY-FIVE

MENDES AND HIS COVEN'S BOLT HOLE TURNED OUT TO BE an eight-thousand-square-foot, opulent, Tuscan-style mansion hidden amidst thirty acres of private woodland two miles from the church. Manicured gardens stretched from the trees south of the estate to a swimming pool and terrace at the back of the property.

"This is a pretty fancy hideout," Nikolai grunted.

"Bryony did say the guy was loaded," Mae muttered.

"It's probably a rental," Vlad observed.

"Can you tell where he is?" Cortes asked Mae.

Mae had used *Reveal* on one of the bloodied feathers they'd found in the church to locate the harpy eagle. What she hadn't told the others yet was what she'd picked up on during that spell. She frowned.

"Mendes is in the master suite on the second floor, at the rear of the property. The bird's with him. The rest of his coven are spread across the first floor."

"Are there any black magic users among them?" Violet asked nervously.

"No."

"That's always a bonus," Vlad muttered.

Cortes narrowed his eyes. "How should we do this?"

Mae pursed her lips. "Something tells me these guys won't listen to reason."

Vlad clenched his jaw. "Because they're working for the Dark Council?"

Mae shook her head. "Because they're scared out of their minds, just like they were back at the reception."

The others stared.

"I can smell the fear saturating their cores from here," she said in a hard voice.

"Does that mean the Dark Council is forcing them to act against their will?" Nikolai asked in a troubled voice.

"Probably. I think we should—"

Mae froze. Something had just brushed against her magic. Her scalp prickled.

It was an echo of what she'd detected during *Reveal*.

Brimstone growled. *We need to hurry, my witch!*

"What is it?" Violet asked tensely.

Mae jumped to her feet. "We don't have much time! You guys take care of the coven. I'll handle Mendes and the harpy eagle!"

Brimstone jumped on her shoulder as she rose inside a red sphere of power.

"Mae!" Vlad called out, alarmed.

Mae twisted around and met their worried gazes.

"I'll meet you inside! Make sure you don't hurt the coven!"

She shot across the grounds, her attention focused on the unstable magic she could feel pulsing inside the mansion.

The harpy eagle's core was minutes away from imploding.

Dammit, I hope we're not too late!

It will be faster if we go through the roof, my witch! Brimstone said.

Mae nodded briskly. "Hell, you're up!"

Hellreaver detached from her neck and transformed.

They slowed to a hover where the bird's unbalanced power throbbed the strongest. Crimson erupted around Hellreaver. He dropped and carved out a hole in the roof and the floor of the attic space below it.

A violent outburst of magic raised the hairs on Mae's arms when they descended inside the suite. Brimstone leapt off her shoulder and transformed as she alighted on the floor.

Mendes's head whipped around. He was trying to contain the screeching harpy eagle inside a cage of Arcane Magic. Horror widened the High Priest's eyes. Gold bloomed in the pupils of the black hare at his feet.

Mendes turned and cast a spell bomb at them. He cursed when Hellreaver sliced through it in a flash.

Someone shouted in the distance. The sorcerer's startled gaze cut to the door. The sound of fighting and detonating spell bombs could be heard rising from the floor below.

"Look, we don't want to hurt you or your people!" Mae told Mendes urgently. "But if you don't let me help, she won't survive what's happening to her!"

Her belly twisted when she glanced at the harpy eagle. The bird's core was close to cracking.

Spell bombs burst into life before the panic-stricken Mendes. The hare hissed as he augmented his sorcerer's magic.

Mae cursed and unleashed *Devour.* "Brim!"

"*On it,*" the demon fox growled.

Devour swallowed the sorcerer's attacks with gluttonous gulps. Mendes took a step back and clenched his jaw defiantly. His hare bared his teeth at the demon fox looming over them.

"*Shield!*" the sorcerer barked.

"*Absorb!*" Mae countered.

Her spell consumed Mendes's defensive barrier even as it formed. He cried out as Brimstone gently pressed a paw to his chest and backed him all the way to the wall. Hellreaver blocked the hare's path when it made to attack Brimstone.

"Keep them there!"

Mae crossed the floor briskly, her pulse racing. She had seconds left to act.

"No! Please!" Mendes's voice broke where he struggled beneath Brimstone's hold. "Don't—don't kill Sable, I beg of you!"

"I won't." Mae lowered her brows. "I'm going to save her." Power thrummed across her bond with Brimstone and Hellreaver. "*Absorb!*"

Mendes's Arcane Magic spell wavered. The cage

started to disperse as her magic ate away at it. The harpy eagle's mad gaze swiveled to the hole in the roof, her wings bunching and quivering as she prepared to launch into an escape.

"Contain!"

The bird screeched when she found her flight path blocked by Mae's crimson prison. She scratched and batted at the barrier in a frenzy, heedless of her damaged claws and the blood seeping onto her feathers.

Mae's heart thumped heavily as she pressed her hands to *Contain*. Her gaze met that of the enraged bird briefly before she closed her eyes and focused on the wrongness within the maddened familiar.

The bird's dull core appeared in her mind's eye.

Ice filled her veins when she finally saw what she'd felt back at the church when she'd used *Reveal*.

Dark runes had been scored inside the creature.

It's black magic, alright. But why couldn't Nullify *show it to me before?!*

The stench of corruption had faded to a whiff probably only she could discern. Dread sent a shiver dancing down her spine when she picked up on a distinctive undertone to the spell. It was one she'd encountered once before.

Vedran! Mae clenched her jaw. *Shit! Have Barquiel and Dietrich found a way to hide the Dark Council's magic from me?! Or it this one of Vedran's abilities?!*

"What is it, my witch?" Brimstone growled.

She opened her eyes. "The Dark Council has overwritten her bond with her magic user!"

A feral sound left Brimstone. Hellreaver whined angrily.

Their fury resonated with Mae's. The reason for the harpy eagle's unpredictable behavior was now clear. She had gone insane from having her original bond forcibly suppressed and her soul bound to the will of another.

Mae didn't have to make an educated guess as to who the culprit was. The rest of the spell stank of his power.

That bastard Oscar!

She recalled what Nikolai and Vlad had reported about their fight with the Sorcerer King's heir on Staten Island. That he'd grown stronger, thanks to his father's magic.

Her belly grew hot as she reached for her magic. The room filled with a scarlet light that made the windows tremble and sent her hair fluttering around her face.

"Negate!"

Her power clashed against Oscar and Vedran's spell. Mae grunted as the collision pushed her back a step. She ground her teeth and dug her heels into the floor.

Some of the runes started to fade. The rest resisted *Negate.*

The harpy eagle screeched.

Dread brought a sour taste to the back of Mae's mind. *She'll die if I keep going!*

She retracted the spell and swallowed, her mind racing frantically.

I need to protect her core until I can figure out how to undo Oscar and Vedran's magic! But how?! Think, Mae!

She focused on the infinite grimoire locked inside her mind, bringing forth and casting aside spells she knew and some she was yet to invoke. One caught her attention.

She had only used it once before.

It might work!

Mae took a deep breath. *"Soul Conjure!"*

The sound of agony that left the harpy eagle made her bite her lip and had Brimstone grunting in sympathy. The bird convulsed for long seconds inside *Contain* before going motionless. A pale orb floated out of her body as she levitated limply within Mae's prison.

Mendes sagged. "Oh God! You've killed her!"

He covered his face and sobbed. His hare whimpered at his side.

Brimstone lowered his head and nudged Mendes with his nose. *"Calm down, sorcerer. The bird is not dead."*

Nikolai and Vlad burst through the suite door. "Mae!"

They rocked to a halt, their eyes rounding. Cortes appeared behind them, Violet and Miles on his heels. The three of them froze behind the sorcerer and the incubus.

"Shit." Violet swallowed heavily. "Is that *Soul Conjure?!*"

"Yes." Mae's insides twisted as she ended *Contain.* She caught the harpy eagle and cradled her gently to her chest. The creature's racing heart began to settle, as did the quivering orb that was her soul. "It's okay," she mumbled. "You're okay, now."

Cortes stared at the pale globe floating next to the bird. "You conjured the soul of a living creature?"

"Her core would have cracked otherwise," Mae said quietly.

Cortes paled. She knew he was thinking about his first familiar.

She studied Sable with a faint frown.

She had no doubt Oscar would have felt his authority over the familiar shatter wherever he was right now. Whether he would think it was because she'd died was another matter.

Mae wrapped the bird and her inert soul within a protective shield before turning to an ashen-faced Mendes. "We should talk."

CHAPTER TWENTY-SIX

that demon came to our city twelve days ago and
attacked our coven before kidnapping her."

Mendes stared blindly at his hands where they sat
in the mansion's main sitting room.

Mae's heartbeat accelerated. The pieces of the
puzzle were finally falling into place. "Does Anya have
blonde hair and gray eyes?"

Mendes recoiled like she'd struck him.

Her chest tightened. Mendes looked like a broken
man. There was little doubt in her mind now that the
swagger he and his coven had demonstrated at the
reception had been to hide their fear.

"How do you know that?" Mendes whispered
thinly.

Troubled murmurs broke out among the members
of his coven. Though most of them still watched her
and the others with deep mistrust, it was clear they

were petrified of how the Dark Council might react to their current situation.

Mendes's aide spoke up. "This is a bad idea, Sergio. You know what they'll do to Anya if they find out we're talking to the Witch Queen!"

The sorcerer's strained gaze flitted to the red sphere bobbing next to Mae. Sable and her soul orb floated peacefully inside it.

Mendes ignored his aide and glowered at Mae, color returning to his face. "Answer me!"

"I saw a vision of your daughter when I went back to where I triggered her mirage magic."

Mendes drew a sharp breath. His chin wobbled. "You saw Anya?!"

"Yes."

Hope brightened the High Priest's face. "Did—did she seem okay?!"

Mae hesitated. "She was alive."

Mendes's expression crumpled. His aide fisted his hands, his distress and that of his coven plain to see. Anya was clearly loved by them all.

"Illusion Sorcery," Mendes mumbled.

Mae straightened.

Mendes swallowed heavily before meeting her gaze. "That's the name of Anya's magic. It's called Illusion Sorcery. There are only a handful of people in the world who possess it."

"The Sorcerer King sure likes collecting rare things," Cortes said bitterly in the fraught hush.

Mae's stomach tightened. *He's right. First Roman and now Anya. It seems Vedran is keen on amassing formidable talent at his side. Whether they wish to join him doesn't seem to factor in the equation.* Her nails dug into her palms as she cut her eyes to Nikolai. *His mother was one of them. And now, so is he. Is this all because he wishes to defeat me?*

The burden of her destiny weighed heavily upon her shoulders at that moment. So many lives had been impacted by the war Vedran and his Dark Council had chosen to bring to her door.

Hellreaver whined against her chest. *This isn't your fault, my witch.*

Brimstone pressed against her leg. *He is right.*

Their words warmed her heart and strengthened the resolve that had been born inside her the night she had awakened. A puzzling question had her frowning at Mendes.

"How come Anya can maintain that spell without Sable?"

"Sable was with her at the time she was forced to conjure the Illusion Sorcery," Mendes explained bitterly. "Oscar separated them afterward and sent Sable to New York with us so we could obtain a sample of your blood. I suspect that vile man is maintaining her magic with the Dark Council's own foul power."

Mae's mouth went dry as another segment of the puzzle fell into place.

So, that's why it was Sable who scratched me and not someone from Mendes's coven! Because she's Anya's familiar and could directly feed my blood to her witch!

"I saw a barrier around Anya in that vision," she told Mendes grimly. "I presumed it was to guard her, but it must be powering her core so she can maintain the Illusion Sorcery."

Unease clouded Nikolai's face. "It would explain that eerie feeling we had in the church."

Mae focused on Mendes once more. "Am I correct in presuming Illusion Sorcery is only meant to last until the witch or sorcerer who casts it achieves their goals?" She clenched her fists. "In this instance, that things will return to normal if I die and they take Nikolai back?"

Violet sucked in air.

Vlad glowered and shot to his feet. "What?!"

Cortes stared at Mae. "I thought this was about making the world of magic forget about you."

"Since they can't capture me alive, I think they've decided they'd rather have me dead than wandering around like a time bomb that might come after them at any given moment. And they want to study my corpse." Mae tapped her left temple with a finger. "Specifically what's in here."

Redness bloomed in Vlad's eyes. His anguish sent a pulse of demonic energy washing across the room. "How can you say that so calmly? Don't you know how many people will grieve your passing? Is your heart made of stone, my queen?!"

Tarang whimpered, ears pressing against his skull. Violet and Miles paled as the incubus's angry words rang across the room.

Cortes reached out and squeezed Vlad's arm. "Calm down."

Vlad scowled, knuckles white at his side.

Mae met his tormented stare unflinchingly. "They killed me once before."

Vlad recoiled.

Her expression softened. "It's not that I take my life lightly. It's just that I see things more...objectively now. Though I was an infant when the first Sorcerer King and Barquiel killed me, I remember every single thing they did to my parents and my people. Crying about what they intend to do to me again will achieve nothing." She smiled flintily. "I'd rather turn those emotions into action and crush their balls."

Mendes spoke in the fraught hush.

"I'm afraid you're wrong," he told Mae in a strained voice. "The only way to end Illusion Sorcery is for the caster to withdraw the spell from the altar where it was invoked. And it needs to happen before the midnight hour of the next Equinox."

His words sent a chill down her spine. Tension thickened the air.

"Why the next Equinox?" Vlad asked stiffly.

"Because that's when Anya's Illusion Sorcery will be at its peak," Mendes confessed.

"What happens if it isn't undone before then?" Cortes said guardedly.

"Then the illusion will become permanent," Mendes's aide stated bitterly.

Mae's throat tightened. Vlad's mouth pressed into a thin line.

"Shit," Violet mumbled.

Cortes lowered his brows. "When's the next Equinox?"

Mendes sagged. "The Harvest Moon is tonight."

Mae's stomach knotted.

Nikolai looked jerkily out the window. Dawn was leaching the darkness from the horizon. He met her horrified gaze, his own eyes filled with dread.

They had less than twenty-four hours left to find the church and the altar.

Cortes's face tightened as he looked at Mae. "That means the person who helped Raya by invoking the Illusion Sorcery that allowed her to defeat me retracted the spell of their own free will. Or else my family would never have regained their memories. Raya would have wanted them to forget about me forever."

Mae's eyes widened. "You're right."

Mendes and his aide traded a confused glance. "What are you talking about?"

Cortes explained how his aunt had tried to get rid of him and killed his first familiar. "Someone we know told us my Arcane Magic protected me, even though my core ended up cracking. And my coven did not seem affected by the Illusion Sorcery that wiped everyone else's memories yesterday this time around."

Mendes drew a sharp breath. "So the rumor is true?" His wild gaze swung to Mae. "You fixed his core?!"

"Nikolai and I did," Mae confirmed with a nod.

Mendes looked blindly at the floor, his shock reverberating through his coven. He lifted his face and observed Cortes cautiously. "To be this powerful again after your core was damaged means you would have been destined to be the strongest Arcane Magic user this world has ever seen."

"I still am," Cortes stated bluntly.

Popo bobbed his head proudly on the sorcerer's shoulder.

"Arcane Magic can indeed protect against Illusion Sorcery," Mendes said. "You just need to know how to wield it against that specific spell. That's why those with the ability to use Illusion Sorcery are born in families with Arcane Magic." He fixed Cortes with a shrewd stare. "It appears your coven found out about the spell they had been under and learned how to counter it in case it ever happened to them again."

Cortes looked discomfited at that.

Nikolai frowned at Mendes. "Why are you hiding from the Dark Council? Aren't you worried about what they might do to Anya?"

"They won't kill Anya," Mendes said bitterly. "She's too precious a commodity for them to cast aside." He glanced at his aide. "Oscar promised Anya her coven wouldn't come to any harm if she did as he asked, but we knew he lied. We overheard one of the Dark Council witches say he was planning to kill us the day after the reception."

A sour taste filled Mae's mouth. The Dark Council's actions should come as no surprise to her.

"I take it you have no idea where they could be holding her?" she asked Mendes.

He shook his head, his expression gaunt.

"The church and the hill," Nikolai said uneasily. "They both vanished as if they never existed. Was that

Illusion Sorcery too or is the Dark Council capable of relocating entire buildings with black magic now?"

Mae suspected he was thinking about *Transmigrate*. As far as they knew, no one in the Dark Council could use that spell. She narrowed her eyes.

Then again, Vedran keeps on surprising us.

"It was the first part of the illusion," Mendes explained reluctantly. "Your blood helped put it together. The full spell only took effect after one of you touched my daughter's magic."

Mae winced. "So, the church was there and it also… wasn't after I activated Anya's magic?"

Mendes nodded. "Reality shifted completely at that moment."

"It hurts my head to even think about it," Violet mumbled.

"What now?" Frustration tightened Vlad's face. "We have less than a day to find a church no one knows about and stop these bastards before their plans come to fruition!"

"I don't know." Nikolai blew out a vexed sigh and ran a hand through his hair. "But we can't just sit around here doing nothing."

"Wherever that church is, there's red clay close by," Mae reminded him.

The sorcerer stilled. "You're right."

Vlad's brow furrowed. "What red clay?"

Mae told them about the footprints they'd found inside the building.

Cortes's expression grew pinched. "That still doesn't help narrow things down."

Mae grimaced. "I know." She looked over at Sable. "We need to do something about her first." She chewed her lip before looking over at Nikolai. "I have an idea. I don't know if it will work, but it's worth a try."

"What?" Nikolai said warily.

"I want to use our magic to erase the spell Vedran and Oscar put inside her."

CHAPTER TWENTY-SEVEN

"You want to do what?!" Mendes said hoarsely.

Nikolai held Mae's gaze, his pulse racing. "You mean, how you channeled your magic through my core and Roman's in Prague?"

She nodded. "Kinda. But I'm going to try and fuse our powers this time, rather than just use you as a conduit. I need your white magic."

Vlad narrowed his eyes, evidently not liking the sound of that one bit.

Nikolai hesitated. Though he understood her perspective on the current situation, he shared Vlad's feelings on the subject to a certain extent. Mae's actions had become increasingly reckless as of late whenever Barquiel was involved. Guilt stabbed through him.

Is it because of Rose?

He hesitated before clenching his jaw. "Okay. If it can help save her."

"She can channel other people's magic through their cores?" Mendes asked Cortes numbly.

Cortes made a face. "She can see other people's cores without even trying."

Mendes's aide blanched.

"We should probably do this outside," Mae said.

Nikolai followed her out onto the terrace behind the mansion, the others trailing in their wake. His breath misted in the cool pre-dawn air. Vivid orange and pink streaks had started to lighten the sky to the east.

Sable's magic containment floated beside Mae as they stopped some fifty feet from the residence, the familiar oblivious to everything around her.

Mae moved the bird in front of him.

"Put your hands on the sphere," she instructed.

Alastair shifted closer as Nikolai did as he was told. The heat of Mae's magic danced against his palms, as familiar as his own breath.

"I'm going to show you the spell inside Sable." Mae walked behind him and placed her hands on his back. "*Negate* will kill her. So, we'll have to work together to create a conjuration that can undo Vedran and Oscar's magic without harming her core."

Nikolai swallowed, his pulse quickening. "How?"

"I'll give you access to what's inside my head. If something resonates with you, reach for it."

Nikolai froze. He jerked his head around and met Mae's calm gaze. "You can do that?!"

"We won't know until we try."

If Mae was aware of his hesitation, she didn't show

it. She addressed the others. "You guys had better move back." She grimaced. "And put your shields up just to be safe."

Brightly colored barriers brightened the twilight. A scarlet veneer engulfed Vlad and Tarang as they stepped away to a safe distance.

Brimstone and Hellreaver transformed.

Their magic washed across Nikolai and Alastair in a crimson wave as they merged their powers with Mae.

"Are you ready?" Mae said in a steely voice.

Nikolai drew on his core. Heat warmed his belly. Power flooded his veins and thrummed across his bond with Alastair. A pale haze of white magic and Moon Magic fluttered to life around them.

"I'm ready."

Mae's hands grew hot against his back. He gasped when her magic blasted into his core scant seconds later. Red roared and clashed with white, a maelstrom that made his blood boil and his entire body go rigid. He clenched his teeth and grunted.

This was different from the instances in Prague when Mae had used him to end the storm of Hellfire that had threatened to destroy the city and to close the crack in the nexus.

"Breathe!" Mae urged. "Stop fighting me!"

Cold air wheezed through Nikolai's windpipe as he gulped. He hadn't realized he'd been holding his breath. Alastair's feathers rustled next to his ear, the crow amplifying their magic so they could accept the power of the Witch Queen.

The storm inside him slowly stabilized. Nikolai

blinked. Something had just flickered across his inner vision. It took a couple of heartbeats to figure out what it was.

I—I can see my core!

A blazing orb filled his mind's eye. Half of it was made of incandescent white light. The other half glowed with the power of the sun itself, so strong it seared his senses.

This is Mae's magic?!

The perspective changed with a speed that made him draw a sharp breath.

He felt his consciousness dive through Mae's *Contain* and into the harpy eagle. For a moment, all he could see was darkness. The gloom started to lighten up ahead. A familiar corruption touched his magic as the shadows faded.

His heart stuttered.

There, deep within the body of the familiar, was a dull core covered in half-faded black runes. His throat tightened when he detected the stench of the Sorcerer King's power, along with that of his brother.

Mae's touch burned into his flesh.

"Here we go!" she warned between clenched teeth.

Nikolai heard a distant boom above the sound of his thundering heart. He knew from the intense pulsation in his core that she'd just released the cap on her magic.

The infinite repertoire she had inherited by virtue of her birth exploded before his eyes. He swallowed. Hundreds upon hundreds of runes drifted across his vision, some barely perceptible, as if they were floating inside a deep, dark sea.

"I don't know how much longer I can keep this up!" Mae shouted.

Sweat beaded Nikolai's forehead. He gritted his teeth. *I need to focus!*

He tapped into the spell surrounding Sable's core and watched Mae's limitless magic roll before his mind's eye.

Something flashed in the gloom. Nikolai's breath caught. Alastair crooned softly.

There!

He dove inside the vast ocean that was Mae's subconscious and grasped at the pale rune he and Alastair had just spotted. It resisted his hold for a moment. Another bright flash lit up the shadows on his left. He frowned and swam toward it.

It felt like forever had passed by the time he had all the runes in his clutches.

He studied them for long seconds before weaving them into a spell. He had never seen it before but he knew inherently what its power could do. The white-red core inside him brightened as he drew on his and Mae's fused magic. His chest swelled on his next inhale. He felt Mae take a deep breath.

Their combined voices rang sweetly in his ears as they invoked the conjuration.

"PURGE!"

The light that scorched the dark runes from Sable's core filled his world. Black spots swarmed his vision.

Shouts reached him faintly above the buzzing in his ears. The ground quaked beneath his feet.

Mae steadied him, her touch unshakable.

Nikolai's heart pounded heavily when he felt her end *Soul Conjure*. Light filled the murky interior of Sable's body as her soul reappeared and sank inside her core.

There was a moment's stillness during which both he and Mae held their breath.

Brightness pulsed through the bird's core. It detonated with blazing blue flames that lit up the space around it.

Mae sagged against his back. "Thank God!"

Nikolai shuddered as she unfused their magic and lifted her hands off his back. He reached blindly behind him and grasped her wrist, not wanting to let go of this intimate moment. Her fingers slipped into his grasp and twined around his.

His vision flickered. His sight returned. The terrace and gardens blurred into view.

It took a moment for him to grasp what he was seeing.

"Shit," he mumbled.

"Yeah, well, it couldn't be helped," Mae muttered.

Brimstone and Hellreaver huffed, clearly unrepentant.

Giant cracks had torn across the estate, uprooting bushes and trees and even a pergola. All the glass this side of the mansion had been blown to smithereens. Half of Mendes's coven looked to have been blasted onto their backs by the power of the spell despite their shields and were slowly getting back onto their feet.

Vlad watched them warily from behind Cortes's Arcane Magic barrier.

"Is it over?" the incubus asked.

Nikolai's gaze swept the destruction he and Mae had unleashed. "Yeah."

Violet sagged and retracted her shield alongside an ashen-faced Miles.

"Next time, we'll just leave you guys to it and go to the next town," the sorcerer grumbled.

Mendes's eyes rounded. "Sable!"

He hurried over, his hare loping at his side.

Nikolai looked around.

The harpy eagle was awake and floating serenely inside *Contain*.

Mae ended the spell. Sable fluttered onto her shoulder. She studied Mae for a moment before nuzzling her cheek lovingly.

Brimstone's hackles rose slightly. The harpy eagle ignored the fox and started grooming Mae's hair with her beak.

"That tickles," Mae chuckled.

Sable looked around and crooned softly at the sight of Mendes.

"Sable," the High Priest mumbled tearily.

He lifted a trembling arm. The bird hopped onto his wrist. Her eyes shrank to happy slits as he gently stroked her head, the hare hopping excitedly at his feet.

Nikolai turned to Mae. "I figured out the spell Vedran and Oscar put inside her."

Mae startled. "You did?"

He scowled. "It's called *Subjugate*."

CHAPTER TWENTY-EIGHT

"The Harvest Moon?" Mrs. Son-Ha made a face. "You mean Mabon?" She waved a celery stick at them. "You people believe in that stuff?"

Violet gave the old woman a leaden look as she made them coffee. "You're asking that question after everything you've seen?"

Mrs. Son-Ha popped the celery stick in her juicer along with several other vegetables. "There are a lot of quacks out there. It's best not to believe everything you hear."

She pressed the button on the machine.

Cortes watched the green liquid sloshing around the inside of the juicer. "I hope that's not our breakfast."

"You and me both," Jared murmured.

Since they couldn't trust what the New York coven would do to the Immortal, they'd asked Mrs. Son-Ha if he could spend the night at her place.

Mrs. Son-Ha rolled her eyes and indicated her oven. "I made *Hoeddeok* for you guys."

Jared brightened.

"It's a pancake with cinnamon, honey, and peanuts," Mae explained at Cortes's blank look. "You'll like it."

Jared turned to Vlad. "How about you get one of your lackeys to bring us some pastries from *Vetriano?*"

Vlad's expression grew cool. "First of all, my men aren't lackeys. Secondly, I hate to break it to you, but it looks like the Illusion Sorcery wiped *Vetriano's* reputation clean. I already checked. It looks like they closed months ago."

"No way!" Jared gasped. He lowered his brows. "Those Dark Council bastards."

"Vlad gets breakfast pastries from *Vetriano?*" Mrs. Son-Ha asked Nikolai while the Immortal said a few more choice curse words.

"He's one of their top clients," the sorcerer grunted.

Sable crooned softly where she perched on the windowsill with Popo and Alastair. The parrot and the crow were trying to cheer her up.

To Mae's relief, the brightness of Sable's core had intensified since their return to Glendale. She suspected Anya's bond with her familiar had been re-established. Which meant the witch knew the bird was no longer under the control of *Subjugate.*

Mae had asked Mendes if they could keep Sable with them before they'd left East Brunswick. She was convinced the familiar would be crucial to Anya's fight with the black magic still subduing her. Mendes had reluctantly agreed before setting off with his coven to another secret location. Since there was a chance the powerful magic signature Mae and Nikolai had left at the estate would attract the attention of the New York coven, they'd decided it would be best if they left East Brunswick.

Alicia appeared halfway through breakfast. "Bryony and Abraham are scouring the city looking for you guys." She frowned at Jared. "You've made their list of suspects. There's a warrant out for you."

Jared swallowed a mouthful of *Hoeddeok*. "Shit."

Cortes's phone pinged. He stiffened when he looked at the display. "I have to make a call."

He rose and disappeared, Dexter yipping around his feet.

Popo eyed the peanuts on Cortes's plate.

"Don't do it," Violet warned.

"What Enrique doesn't know won't hurt him," the parrot said confidently.

He'd just leaned over to steal some nuts when his sorcerer walked back into the room.

Cortes stopped and narrowed his eyes. "You like living on the edge, don't you?"

Popo dropped his spoils guiltily.

"You're an idiot," Violet told the parrot.

"The Medellin coven has found someone with knowledge of Raya's entourage at the time she was growing her support in secret to try and take over my family's territory," Cortes reported in a hard voice. "The guy moved from the city ten years ago. They're tracking him down right now. We should have a list of names in a few hours."

Mae's stomach churned. She could tell Vlad and Nikolai had just had the same thought from their darkening faces. They were running out of time to locate the church.

But the list, when it finally came, turned out to be an obituary.

Mae stared at the names Cortes had penned out on a piece of paper.

"They're all dead?" she repeated numbly.

"I'm sorry." Cortes ran a hand through his hair, his brow furrowed and a muscle ticking in his cheek. "It looks like Raya had a clean-up right after she tried to kill me. She probably didn't want to leave any witnesses behind."

Vlad cursed.

Mae's heart sank. She'd been banking on the insight of the person who'd conjured up the Illusion Sorcery that had aided Raya in defeating Cortes to help locate Anya.

Alicia lowered her brows. "But didn't you say you thought the person who helped Raya with that magic undid it without her knowing? That means someone got away, doesn't it?"

Mae's pulse quickened. She met Cortes's startled gaze. "She's right."

Nikolai studied the obituary with narrowed eyes. "One of them must have faked their death."

"It wouldn't be the first time someone tried something like that," Cortes grunted.

Violet chewed her lip and looked over at Jared.

"Should we tell you-know-who to run that list through his database?"

Mae stared. "Who the heck is you-know-who?"

Violet hesitated. "A friend of our allies in Chicago."

Jared's mouth flattened into a thin line. "Do you mean the idiot on the West Coast or the one in the Czech Republic?"

The witch shrugged. "Either." She looked at the clock. "Howard should be up."

Miles blinked. "Why do you know Howard's timetable?"

Violet flushed and avoided his gaze. "Because we're friends."

Suspicion narrowed Miles's eyes. "You're not cheating on Erik, are you?"

"No," Violet protested. She turned to Jared. "Call Howard."

"That's assuming that playboy didn't go to some glitzy party last night and isn't in bed with a woman," Jared scoffed.

Violet sighed. "Just call him."

"That won't be necessary," Alicia said.

Nikolai arched an eyebrow. "It won't?"

"Give me a moment."

A cool breeze swirled around the kitchen as the Reaper Queen transformed.

Mrs. Son-Ha sucked in air. It was her first time seeing Alicia's true form. Her dogs whimpered and bolted behind her, bodies quivering and tails drooping.

Alicia manifested her scythe and touched the list of

names with the sharp end of her weapon. Crimson flared in her orbits.

Mae's mouth went dry. Some of the lines on the paper were brightening with an eerie, white light while others turned a fiery black. Only one name did not change.

Alicia tapped it with a bony finger. "There's your suspect."

"Do you think you can find this person?" Mae asked hopefully.

Alicia shifted back to her human form. "Like I said before, needle, haystack. Unless they're on death's door and about to cross over, neither I nor my reapers can locate their soul."

"That wasn't creepy at all, by the way," Jared told Alicia leadenly.

The Reaper Queen rolled her orbits. She caught Mrs. Son-Ha's bright stare. "What?"

"Can you teach me how to do that?" their host said zealously.

Jared took his cell out while the Reaper Queen explained to the Shaman why that would be a bad idea. He brought up a number, hit dial, and met Mae's puzzled stare with a frown. "Between Howard and Jordan, we should have a location in a couple of hours."

Mae stepped out into the back yard a while later, too tense to stay in the house. Mrs. Son-Ha had assured her the barrier would keep them hidden from curious eyes. She shivered a little as she leaned her elbows on the rear porch railing.

The temperature had started to drop. Autumn would soon give way to winter.

Something in the sky caught her eye.

The Harvest Moon was already visible, an orange hue lighting up its southern hemisphere. Mae chewed her lip and wondered if its presence would make Nikolai's magic stronger.

The door clattered open behind her. Nikolai crossed the porch and propped his elbows on the railing next to her.

A companionable silence settled between them.

"You reckon those white and dark lights Alicia raised with her scythe meant Heaven and Hell?" the sorcerer said after a while.

Mae grimaced. "Probably."

She turned and leaned backward on the railing.

"What you did back in East Brunswick? That was pretty incredible," he said quietly.

Mae glanced at him. "That was on both of us. I couldn't have done it without you."

Nikolai smiled faintly. "We make a good team."

Her mouth curved. "We do."

The silence between them thickened. Mae shivered, this time for a whole other reason. The desire that lay ever dormant between them sparked the air. Nikolai turned and closed the distance between them with a single step, his heated gaze raking her face as if he were looking for an answer to a question only he knew.

Mae's breath quickened when he lifted a hand and caressed her cheek with his knuckles.

"Choose me," he whispered. "I will make you happy."

Mae swallowed. Her gaze dropped to his lips.

Nikolai's eyes grew hooded. He slipped a hand behind her neck and lowered his head to take her mouth in a kiss that made her soul hum. Mae sank into him with a sound of pure need, her arms rising to lock around his nape. He groaned, clasped her face, and angled her head so he could deepen the kiss.

The door creaked open on a forceful swing. They froze.

"We found her! She's in—"

Vlad rocked to a halt when he saw them.

Mae disengaged herself awkwardly from Nikolai, unable to stop the guilt that twisted her insides.

Nikolai's face grew inscrutable as he met Vlad's hostile stare. "I'll get ready to leave."

He walked past the incubus and entered the house. Mae hesitated before following.

"Have you chosen, princess?" Vlad said in a stilted voice when she drew level with him.

Mae's chest tightened at the bitterness underlying his words. "I—" She faltered and bit her lip. "Vlad—"

"Don't." The incubus shuddered and closed his eyes. "I'd rather you not lie to me."

CHAPTER TWENTY-NINE

THE CLAMOR OF AN EXCITED CROWD WASHED OVER THEM as they stepped out of the SUV they'd rented at the airport. A dull roar preceded the sound of distant clapping to the far left, where a large tent decorated with strings of colorful lights rose against the dark sky.

Mae pulled up the collar of her jacket and tucked her cap down as they crossed the parking lot. Though night had fallen, there was a risk the bright lights illuminating the fairground could expose her identity to curious eyes.

"A circus in Pittsburgh is the last place I'd have thought we'd find this woman," Alicia remarked. "She chose a good hideout."

Mae had to agree. It was unlikely the Dark Council would look for the witch who had escaped Raya Medeiros's death trap here.

They'd ended up having to hire a private charter from one of the smaller airfields outside New York to avoid the attention of the authorities searching for them. The pilot hadn't batted an eyelid when he'd seen the strange get-up of sunglasses, hats, and scarfs Mae and Nikolai had donned, like this was a regular thing for him.

Vlad's mood hadn't improved during their short flight to Pittsburgh, something Cortes and the others had noticed but thankfully not commented upon. Mae knew they needed to talk and soon. She couldn't just leave things as they were.

The incubus meant too much to her.

Violet scanned the sea of booths and stalls around them. The kiosks were spread across three central lanes with about a dozen side alleys branching off each one.

"Should I go ask someone where she is?"

"There's no need," Mae said. "I can sense her core. She's on the far side of the fairground."

"Oh." Violet eyed her dully. "I keep forgetting you can do that."

"Are there any other magic users around?" Nikolai asked guardedly as they navigated the noisy carnival grounds.

"A few," Mae replied. "But none with dark magic. They must belong to the local coven."

"Let's hope they don't cause any trouble," Violet murmured.

The hubbub died down when they turned into a passage next to a muddy field where the circus staff had parked their trailers and trucks. From the looks of the shabby stalls and booths they passed, this was where the least popular gigs were located.

Mae's gaze landed on a rundown purple tent at the end. There was a small queue outside it. Faded, gold lettering announced the title of the booth: *"Lady Luna, Seer of Secrets."*

This close up, the blue flames that characterized the core of the witch and the cat familiar inside it blazed even more brightly. Mae frowned.

She's definitely someone who can use Illusion Sorcery.

They earned a few curious stares as they got in line.

Mae glanced at the orange orb in the sky. The Harvest Moon would reach its peak in just under two hours. Five minutes passed. She crossed her arms and started tapping a foot.

"Stop doing that," Alicia muttered. "You're making me antsy."

Another five minutes passed. A couple exited the tent. Three giggling college girls took their place. The queue shuffled forward.

Mae frowned. "This is taking too long."

Sable crooned worriedly on her shoulder.

Do you want me to bite them? Brimstone suggested.

I can make mincemeat out of them in a flash, my witch, Hellreaver contributed spiritedly. *Just say the word!*

Mae clenched her jaw. She knew what she was about to do was reckless but they couldn't afford to waste any more time.

"I've got a better idea."

She unleashed a subdued version of *Wind Fury* and stormed toward the tent's entrance.

"Great," Jared said leadenly as people went flying into the muddy field with shocked cries. "Just…great."

"Go, go, Mae!" Popo squawked.

"Don't encourage her!" Cortes snapped.

The tent's opening flapped violently around her when she entered.

Lady Luna, née Gloria Espenoza, stared at her with rounding eyes from where she sat behind a foldable metal table, the tarot cards she was about to deal out frozen in her hands. The black cat on her lap hissed and arched its spine when Brimstone and Tarang padded in after Mae.

The three girls turned.

"Out," Mae ordered coolly.

The first girl scowled. "How about you wait your turn, lady?"

"I'm afraid I'm gonna have to ask you to leave." Jared took out his badge. "This is a police matter."

Girl Number One squinted. "That's an NYPD badge." Her lip curled. "You don't have jurisdiction here."

Her friends smiled triumphantly.

Jared lowered his brows. "What are you, a law student?"

"She is, actually," Girl Number Two retorted.

Number One smiled smugly.

Alicia sighed and showed them her FBI badge. "This should do. Now, scram."

Girl Number Three sneered. "That could be a fake for all we know."

Alicia narrowed her eyes. A cold wind made the tent tremble.

The three girls paled as her form lengthened, their

heads tilting as if on a wire as they looked up and up. The shadows inside the tent raced across the ground and thickened into an inky cloak that wrapped about the Reaper Queen's skeletal form.

A choked gurgle left Gloria. She fell off her chair.

Alicia leaned on her scythe and lowered her face close to the petrified girls staring at her with bulging eyes. Redness bloomed in her orbits. "Will this suffice?"

The three girls screamed and ran out of the tent.

Cortes pinched the bridge of his nose. "Was that strictly necessary?"

Bone clinked as Alicia shrugged. "They were getting on my nerves."

Movement caught Mae's eye. Gloria was escaping through an exit at the rear of the tent.

"*Contain!*" Mae barked.

A curse sounded outside. The tent flaps parted again. Gloria and her cat appeared inside within Mae's prison. They glared at her.

"So you finally found me!" Gloria hissed. Blue spell bombs burst into life above her hands, her eyes and those of her cat brightening with the same light. "Don't think I'll go down without a fight!"

"We're not with the Dark Council if that's what you're worried about," Vlad said coldly.

Gloria faltered, still suspicious. "You're not?"

Cortes took a step forward. "Do you recognize me?"

Gloria stared at the Columbian's hard expression. Her lips parted on a gasp.

The spell bombs in her hands dissipated as the color drained from her face. "It's you!"

Cortes lowered his brows. "So, you really are the one who helped Raya!"

Gloria swallowed. "Look, it wasn't like I had a choice in the matter! She threatened to kill my daughter!"

Cortes stiffened.

Mae stared. *That explains a lot.*

"I don't think she's lying," Alicia observed.

Cortes slowly uncurled his fists, the rage fading from his eyes.

"We're only here to talk," Mae told the haggard witch urgently. "We have no intention of hurting you."

Gloria pursed her lips. "Is it about the Illusion Sorcery they used to make the world forget about you?"

Nikolai frowned. Vlad's eyes shrank to slits.

Mae's belly knotted. *So, she knows about it.*

"Will you run if I end *Contain?*"

"No." Gloria scanned the figures around her with a jaundiced look. "It's not like I'd get far anyway." She eyed the tent's entrance with a frown. "We should switch location."

CHAPTER THIRTY

GLORIA'S TRAILER WAS ON THE FAR SIDE OF THE FIELD next to where her tent had been. The clamor of the fairground faded to a dull drone as they crowded inside and shut the door.

Nikolai noted the careful distance Mae and Vlad maintained from one another as he leaned a hip against the worktop of the tiny kitchen. He didn't know what to make of his feelings on the matter.

On the one hand, he should have been thrilled that they were fighting. But he couldn't bring himself to feel happy about the situation. Not when it was clear they were both hurting from the fresh tension simmering between them.

"So, is that old crone still working for the Dark Council?" Gloria asked as she took a seat at her dining table.

Cortes arched an eyebrow. "You knew she'd joined them?"

Gloria shrugged. "I heard it on the grapevine before I fled the country."

"She's dead."

Gloria froze. Her mouth opened and closed soundlessly. "You—you killed Raya?!"

Cortes dipped his head. "Last month, in Prague." He indicated Vlad. "He helped."

The witch's wide-eyed gaze flitted to the incubus. "I...I didn't know."

Relief and something that looked like elation darted in Gloria's eyes. Considering that fact was only known to the Council of the Moon and the High Council, this hardly came as a surprise. Nikolai frowned.

I doubt she's been keeping up with what's been happening in the world of magic. She's been too busy hiding from my father and Barquiel for that.

"Is your daughter okay?" Mae asked.

Gloria hesitated. "Yes. I hid her somewhere Raya couldn't reach her."

"My father and his council have a way of finding out people's best-kept secrets," Nikolai said thinly.

Gloria's fingers tightened on her cat.

"I know," she retorted bitterly. "But they still seem to think I'm dead, for now. That's why they had to find another witch with the power to use Illusion Sorcery. Otherwise, I'm pretty certain they would have used me."

A strained hush fell inside the trailer.

"How did I trigger the Illusion Sorcery Raya forced you to invoke so she could kill me?" Cortes said stiffly. "I don't recall touching any altar."

Gloria made a face. "Remember the museum she took you to the morning of the day she attacked you?"

A perplexed frown wrinkled Cortes's brow. "But all I did was look at some paintings."

"The top of the altar was the slab of stone you walked across when you entered that building."

Nikolai drew a sharp breath.

Cortes stared. "What?!"

Gloria shrugged. "An altar can be anywhere. It doesn't necessarily have to be inside a church."

Vlad touched Cortes's shoulder. The sorcerer stood with his jaw clenched tight and his hands fisted at his sides.

"The name of the witch they're using is Anya Mendes," Mae said. "She's the daughter of Sergio Mendes, the High Priest of the Rio de Janeiro coven."

Gloria flinched. "She's Sergio's daughter?!"

Mae nodded.

"I take it by that that you know Mendes?" Nikolai observed.

"Yes, I do," Gloria mumbled dazedly. "Arcane Magic and Illusion Sorcery are closely related, after all. Damn it, I hadn't thought of that possibility." The witch chewed her lip with a distracted expression before looking warily at Mae. "Why did you come looking for me?"

"Because I think you can help us find her."

Nikolai exchanged a startled glance with Vlad and Cortes.

They'd never questioned Mae about why she'd been

so adamant to find the witch who had helped Raya. He furrowed his brow.

Can this woman really locate Anya and that church?

To his surprise, Gloria didn't look overly shocked by Mae's assertion. She sighed. "How about you tell me how you triggered the spell in the first place?"

Mae gave her a brief rundown of the events of the last week.

Gloria's expression grew focused when she mentioned their return to Marblehead Neck. "You saw a vision of Anya and the altar when you touched the ground?"

Mae nodded.

Gloria frowned. "They must be really close."

Nikolai's pulse quickened.

"You mean, to the island?!" Mae exclaimed.

Gloria dipped her head. "For you to have had that vision means that church's true location has to be within a ten, maybe twenty-mile radius of where you first saw it. And it's rare for a spell to be fully effective if the original altar is too far away." Her frown deepened. "Mendes is wrong. There are two ways to end an Illusion Sorcery spell. Either the witch or sorcerer who created it has to retract it before the midnight hour of the next full moon. Or someone more powerful than they are needs to break the altar where it was conjured."

Nikolai's eyes widened, his surprise echoed by Mae's stunned look.

"We're two hours from Boston." Vlad's jaw

tightened. "We won't make it there on time. The Harvest Moon will peak in ninety minutes."

"Shit," Violet mumbled.

Mae's shoulders slumped. Brimstone whined next to her.

"That church will be next to a powerful source of magic," Gloria said, undaunted.

Nikolai's stomach lurched at the meaning behind her words.

"Wait." Hope brightened Mae's face. "Do you mean a nexus?!"

Gloria bobbed her head. She cut her eyes to Nikolai. "You should be able to reach that church if you locate it and use that teleportation spell of yours." Lines wrinkled her brow. "Something of Anya's would help you find it faster. That nexus will likely hold a vestige of her magic."

"Oh." Mae blinked. "Sable is Anya's familiar."

She indicated the harpy eagle with a grimace. Gloria sucked in air.

"And I have this stone," Nikolai added awkwardly. He took out the item he'd stolen from Oscar. "It was covered in runes made of blue fire when I first saw it."

Gloria scowled. "Why didn't you start with that, you fools?!"

Jared sighed. Alicia rolled her eyes.

A growl rumbled out of Brimstone's throat. Crimson flared around the fox. He rose from where he'd been lying at Mae's feet.

Tension knotted Mae's shoulders. She turned to

face the door of the trailer, her expression grim. "They've found us."

Gloria paled.

A faint whiff of corruption brushed against Nikolai's senses. His insides twisted.

He recognized the Dark Council's magic.

Hellreaver dropped from Mae's neck and transformed, a red aura coating his blades.

"Raise your shields!" Mae warned. "*Now!*"

Alastair squawked on Nikolai's shoulder as he drew on their magic. Barriers erupted inside the trailer a second before a barrage of black magic spell bombs rocked the vehicle.

CHAPTER THIRTY-ONE

THE DETONATIONS LIFTED THE TRAILER AND SENT IT tumbling across the field. Bile flooded the back of Nikolai's throat when the world started spinning sickeningly around him.

Jared went flying into a wall with a curse. Vlad grunted and Tarang yowled as they were violently knocked about.

"*Levitate!*" Mae barked.

The spinning stopped with a suddenness that drew a gasp from Nikolai and made Jared go green. They found themselves floating inside a protective bubble of Mae's magic even as the trailer continued to roll.

Gloria gaped at the translucent globe surrounding her and her cat.

The aura around Mae thickened. "*Contain!*"

The trailer froze in the grip of her magic.

"Everyone okay?!" she snapped in the ringing silence.

"Yeah," Cortes mumbled.

He hugged Popo to his chest inside *Levitate*. Violet and Miles nodded, pale-faced inside their respective spheres.

Vibrations shook the air as the Dark Council launched another volley of attacks at the vehicle, the explosions muffled by Mae's barrier.

None of them breached her magic.

Mae settled the trailer on the ground and retracted *Levitate*.

"*My witch!*" Brimstone warned.

Mae stiffened.

Nikolai's ears popped as a vile pressure pressed down around them. Goosebumps broke out across his flesh. He followed Mae's gaze to the ceiling.

"Shit!" Vlad cursed.

Gloria looked around wildly. "What is that?!"

Redness bloomed in Alicia's pupils as she transformed. "We have company!"

Giant claws sank through the rear roof of the trailer. It peeled open like it was a can of food. Hellwolves appeared against the starlit sky, drool dripping from exposed fangs and obsidian eyes full of hunger.

A hulking figure with ochre pupils clambered atop the trailer next to them. A circus staff badge swung comically from his crooked neck as his black talons scraped the metal.

Nikolai stared at the dark miasma crowning the creature's head and the torn clothes clinging to his deformed body.

That's a demon! But—how did he and those hellbeasts get past Mae's magic?!

"That asshole must have opened a portal inside my barrier!" Mae growled.

Alicia's eyes flared. "It seems they've learned a new trick."

Gloria pointed a trembling finger at the monsters. "Like, seriously, *what the hell are those?!*"

More demons appeared.

"Hellreaver, she's all yours!" Mae ground out.

The weapon levitated defensively in front of Gloria and her cat as Mae conjured *Contain* to protect them.

A blur of movement to the right caught Nikolai's eye. Something dark and big was lunging toward the window next to him.

A hellboar crashed through and smashed into him in a shower of jagged glass before he could move. Nikolai grunted as he went flying headfirst into a kitchen cabinet. Black spots exploded before his eyes.

Alastair's squawk of rage reached him dimly above the ringing in his skull.

"Nikolai!" Mae shouted.

"I'm—I'm okay!"

He straightened and shook his head dazedly, his heart thundering against his ribs. He scowled at the charging hellboar and drew on his magic.

The beast froze mid-lunge when he stabbed it through the eye with *Moon Spear*.

"We need to take this fight out into the open!" Cortes ducked under a demon's claws and slashed the fiend's throat. "We're sitting ducks in here!"

A tortured groan of metal rent the air in the wake of his words. The roof and walls of the trailer came apart as if they were building blocks.

Jared's knuckles blanched on the holy sword he held. "Looks like you got your wish!"

Nikolai's insides twisted at the sight of the horned, winged figure blocking out a section of the night sky above them. Sable made an angry sound.

Crimson detonated around Mae.

Barquiel smirked, his broadsword in hand. "There you are. I see Azazel's daughter has taken to hiding like a rat."

"How about you not take my father's name in vain, dipshit?!" Mae snapped.

Barquiel flicked a clawed hand and sent the trailer sections crashing into the trucks on the other side of the field.

Gloria's eyes bulged when she saw the horde of hellbeasts and demons surrounding them. The monsters were backed by some dozen Dark Council witches and sorcerers. She fell onto her bottom and backpedaled across what remained of her trailer.

Brimstone shifted into his nine-tailed demon spirit form.

"You will never defeat us, fiend!" he snarled at Barquiel.

The demon archduke sneered. "We shall see about that."

Corruption thickened the air. His figure blurred.

Nikolai blinked, his heart in his throat as he tried to follow the demon's movements.

A harsh grunt left Alicia. The Reaper Queen's scythe sparked against Barquiel's blade where she'd countered his lightning-fast strike before he could reach Mae.

"Go!" Alicia yelled over her shoulder. "We'll keep them occupied!"

"She's right," Violet told Mae grimly. She glanced at Nikolai. "You need to get out of here and find her!"

Mae met Nikolai's gaze, her expression conflicted.

"*We must leave, my witch.*" Brimstone looked at the moon. "*We're almost out of time.*"

Violet and Miles slammed their hands on the ground. Purple and gold flared brightly around them and their familiars. The divine power they had inherited from their friends in Chicago mixed with their magic to form a pale wall that blocked the barrage of spell bombs the Dark Council cast their way.

Light bloomed on Jared's sword. He stabbed the blade into the base of Violet and Miles's shield and strengthened the defensive barrier with the heavenly energy within the weapon.

Barquiel roared in rage where he struggled against Alicia.

Mae rushed over to Gloria and ended *Contain*. "Tell us what we need to do!"

The witch didn't react, her numb gaze flitting jerkily from the monsters attacking the divine shield to the demon archduke fighting the Reaper Queen.

Mae grabbed her shoulders. "Gloria!"

The witch flinched. She blinked and focused on them.

Resolve brought some color back to her face. "Give me that stone!"

Nikolai hastily handed her the item. Gloria closed her hands around it. Magic flared between her palms. Nikolai drew a sharp breath when she parted them.

Blue fire traced out the faded runes once more.

"Use it to find Anya's magic!" She gave the stone to him and looked at Mae. "The eagle's core should help you too!"

Sable crooned worriedly on Mae's shoulder.

Mae nodded and swallowed. Regret darkened her face. "I'm sorry we blew your cover."

Gloria gazed at the Dark Council and Barquiel's monsters.

"It was bound to happen one day." Blue flames lit her pupils as she met Mae's worried gaze. "I'm glad I managed to help you in the end, my queen. Like I said before, I won't go down without a fight." She climbed to her feet and dusted herself off, her cat's pupils glowing at her side. "You need to go with them," she told Cortes briskly. "Anya will be in a weakened state. Your magic can help her."

Cortes dipped his head solemnly.

"I'll come with you," Vlad said in a tone that would brook no opposition. "Oscar must be at that church. It's going to take more than the three of you to defeat him and his army."

Nikolai's chest tightened as he met the incubus's gaze. "Thanks."

Vlad lowered his brows. "Don't thank me yet."

CHAPTER THIRTY-TWO

MAE'S HEART POUNDED AS THE DIZZYING EFFECTS OF *Transmigrate* faded, along with the sounds of the battle they had left behind. Whiteness filled her vision.

It took a moment to make out the rivers of pale magic pouring into the dazzling space around them.

Cortes twisted around slowly. "This is the nexus?"

"Yeah," Vlad muttered.

A worried sound escaped Popo. He shuffled closer to Cortes. "Did we die?"

"*No.*" Brimstone's breath ruffled his feathers. "*We are in a place filled with Ran Soyun's magic.*"

They followed Nikolai as he headed briskly across the limitless space. They were somewhere outside Pittsburgh still.

Remorse tightened Mae's throat when she thought of Violet and the others.

"I hope they're okay," she mumbled.

Vlad glanced at her. "They wouldn't have offered to stay behind if they didn't think they could handle things." His tone hardened. "Besides, Barquiel is bound to return to Oscar's side when he realizes what we're up to."

Hellreaver hummed next to her. *He's right, my witch.*

Nikolai stopped and frowned at the ground. "This should do."

He squatted, took out the stone Gloria had infused with her magic, and pressed it against the nexus.

Mae crouched beside him and lifted Sable off her shoulder. "How do we do this?"

A muscle jumped in his jawline as he met her gaze. "I'll need you to connect my powers to her core, like you did before."

"Okay."

Nikolai touched Sable's chest. The harpy eagle stilled, as if she knew what they intended to do. Mae steeled herself and laid her fingers on the sorcerer's back.

Whiteness detonated in Nikolai and Alastair's eyes and around them, the power pulsing off them so strong it made her clothes and hair flutter. Mae's breath froze when she felt their incandescent magic connect to the nexus. She focused and linked them to Sable's core.

Blue fire crackled into life under Nikolai's hand. The flames spread across the ground in jagged lines. Vlad and Cortes observed the phenomenon with cautious looks where they braced to withstand the storm roaring around the nexus.

Sweat beaded Nikolai's forehead. His expression grew glazed as he hunted for an echo of the power he was infusing into the ley lines that spread for thousands upon thousands of miles beneath the Earth.

Mae could feel the tension tightening his body like a spring. She swallowed.

The sorcerer had grown stronger since his return from Prague. She suspected he would be able to bring down Oscar on his own if he were to face him now.

Nikolai froze. "Found it!" Relief made him sag for an instant. His gaze darted to Mae and the two men beside her. "Get ready! This one's going to be bumpy!"

Mae ground her teeth. Fire warmed her belly as she strengthened her bond with Brimstone and Hellreaver. She felt Vlad and Cortes do the same with their familiars.

Nikolai inhaled deeply. "TRANSMIGRATE!"

A whooshing noise filled Mae's ears as they were sucked into the nexus. Dazzling light flickered before her eyes for what felt like an infinite moment, the vortex dragging at her limbs and stealing the breath from her lungs.

Her ears popped when they emerged under an angry sky dominated by a blood moon. Mae blinked and staggered before steadying herself.

The desolate red plain she'd seen in her vision stretched out before them. Her scalp prickled when she spotted the forked tree to their right. She whirled around, her feet squelching in rust-colored mud.

The land sloped upward to form the hill she and Nikolai had last seen on Marblehead Neck. Lightning brightened the heavens. A boom of thunder accompanied the dazzling radiance.

The afterglow outlined the dark church at the top.

"We have twenty minutes left!" Vlad yelled.

They ran up the rise, Tarang and Brimstone loping ahead in a haze of demonic power.

"Enrique, you're with me! We're going to rescue Anya!" Mae glanced at Nikolai and Vlad, her heart racing. "You two take the main altar!"

Black magic thickened the air as they crested the hill. The front doors of the church exploded outward on a hail of spell bombs.

"*Eclipse!*" Mae roared.

"*Moon Storm!*" Nikolai barked.

The black void sucked in the Dark Council's attacks while the white magic wave picked off the witches and sorcerers emerging from the church and sent them flying back inside the building.

Oscar climbed over the bodies of his groaning subordinates, fury darkening his face and Drabek spitting wildly at his side. He pointed his black-magic-wreathed sword at them.

"ROT!"

Brimstone's tails whined, the demonic force that lived in his core resisting the vault of sickening pressure bearing down upon them. Hellreaver stabbed into the dirt with an angry sound. Nikolai's legs buckled. Vlad and Cortes cursed and dropped down on one knee.

Mae clenched her teeth as her legs sank ankle-deep into the red silt. She could taste the power of the Sorcerer King in Oscar's magic, just as Nikolai and

Vlad had described. Fire bubbled through her veins. The mud around her legs started to steam.

"NEGATE!"

Oscar cursed as the spell blasted away at *Rot*. *Wind Fury* swallowed his protest and lifted him and Drabek off their feet in a frenzied whirlwind that carried them all the way down the hill.

Mae scaled the steps to the porch with Nikolai and the others. Barquiel's corruption rocked the building as they dashed inside the church. They stumbled through the quaking vestibule.

Mae's stomach plummeted. A giant portal split the air some twenty feet above the nave to their left. The demon archduke appeared ahead of a horde of hellbeasts. His furious gaze locked on her while the monsters dropped down onto the pews, his wrath practically making the air boil.

A feral sound left Brimstone as black lightning buzzed into life above Barquiel. Sable squawked angrily, blue fire brightening her eyes.

Mae's breath stuttered. Alicia rifted behind the demon, her orbits glinting and her scythe looming under the blood-red moon as she swung it at his back. Barquiel grunted and lurched, the weapon striking the dark scales protecting his flesh in a shower of sparks.

Mae glanced at the gloom-filled chancel. There was an opening in the floor to the right of the obsidian altar.

Her pulse quickened. *That must lead to the basement!*

"Enrique!"

Cortes followed her as she sprinted up the aisle

with Brimstone and Hellreaver, Popo and Sable flying overhead. Nikolai's magic and Vlad's demonic energy washed across their backs as the pair engaged the hellbeasts that threatened to block their path.

The air sizzled above Mae just as she and Cortes reached the chancel. Static lifted her hair around her head and danced across Brimstone's fur and Hellreaver's blades.

Sable screeched out a shrill warning.

Mae grabbed Cortes's arm and took him to the ground with her.

Barquiel's black lightning scored the spot where they'd been a second ago, the explosion so loud Mae thought her eardrums would burst. Broken tile shards rained down around them as they skidded on their front all the way to the entrance to the basement.

Mae activated *Wind Fury* a heartbeat before they tumbled into the drop below the opening. The spell buffered their fall and fetched them up against a moss-covered, stone wall. Brimstone shifted into his smaller form and jumped in after them.

Mae caught him in her arms, twisted around, and raised a hand. *"Eclipse!"*

CHAPTER THIRTY-THREE

A BLACK VOID DETONATED ACROSS THE DOORWAY JUST AS Barquiel flashed into view, Alicia right on his tail. The demon's roar of rage faded to nothingness.

Hopefully that'll keep him busy for a while!

Mae looked at Cortes, her chest heaving with her breaths. "You okay?"

He climbed to his feet and pulled her up. "Never better."

A scarlet glow lit up the gloom beneath them.

Demonic energy wavered around Hellreaver as he growled. *I smell a lot of black magic, my witch!*

Sable settled on Mae's shoulder.

They started rapidly down the winding stairs.

Cortes manifested his blade and whip, the weapons radiating the same golden radiance brightening his and Popo's pupils. "How many?"

Mae counted the cores she could feel below as she unleashed *Devour*. "There's twenty of them."

A savage smile curved Cortes's mouth. "Piece of cake then."

A pair of black magic spell bombs curved up the staircase toward them.

Hellreaver sliced through the attacks in a flash of crimson. *I'll go on ahead, my witch!*

Brimstone scampered after him. *Wait up!*

Mae felt the fox transform seconds before screams echoed beneath them. Brimstone and Hellreaver's powers resonated with her core when she and Cortes reached the bottom of the steps. They rounded a corner and rocked to a halt.

"Fuck," Cortes mumbled.

A horde of Dark Council sorcerers and witches had engaged Hellreaver and Brimstone where they guarded a sickening, translucent black barrier in the middle of the crypt. Enclosed within it was an obsidian pillar blazing with blue runes. Mae's heart raced when her gaze found the blonde bound to the base of the altar.

Anya Mendes looked barely conscious where she hung limply from the shackles biting into her wrists.

Sable released an unholy sound of wrath.

Fury filled Mae's heart. The witch's torn, white dress exposed heavily bruised, cut skin. It was clear she'd been badly tortured.

Magic seared Mae's veins on a crimson wave that pulsed across the basement. It lifted the startled sorcerers and witches fighting Brimstone and Hellreaver off their feet and sent them smashing into the walls.

Sable flew ahead of Mae as she crossed the floor.

Anya lifted her head weakly. Her eyes rounded at the sight of her familiar flapping her wings frenziedly outside the barrier. She froze when she saw Mae. An emotion Mae hadn't expected to see drained what little color the witch possessed from her face. Anya shouted something Mae couldn't make out, her trepidation evident as she struggled against the chains holding her prisoner.

Mae unleashed *Negate* while Cortes, Brimstone, and Hellreaver took care of Oscar's subordinates. The barrier quivered violently when she slammed the spell into it.

It resisted her attack.

She clenched her teeth. She could taste Oscar and Vedran's magic in the wall. Her bond with Brimstone and Hellreaver bloomed with an incandescent, red light as she drew on the power of three.

Mae raised a hand toward Cortes. "*Shield!*"

A scarlet guard detonated in front of a startled Cortes and Popo.

She conjured the next spell on the same breath. "*Absorb!*"

The witches and sorcerers of the Dark Council shuddered and fell to their knees as her spell consumed the magic inside their cores. The black barrier around the pillar wavered and started to dissipate, *Absorb* exhausting the power keeping it up.

Anya's voice finally reached Mae.

"Don't let him touch the altar!" she cried out.

Mae froze. "What?!"

Anya's eyes filled with tears, her expression one of

torment and regret. "There's a second enchantment in the altar meant for Nikolai Stanisic! If he touches the stone, he'll trigger it! Even if the altar breaks, that spell will stay in effect!"

Fear weakened Mae's knees. She swallowed down the panic choking her throat.

"Hellreaver, free her!"

The weapon shot across the basement and carved through the shackles holding Anya to the pillar. The chains clattered to the ground.

Sable flew into her witch's arms.

Anya sobbed and hugged her familiar tightly to her chest. "Sable!" She squeezed her eyes shut briefly before meeting Mae's stricken gaze. "Stop him before he touches the altar! I'll try and retract my magic from down here!"

Mae twisted around. "Enrique, help her!"

Cortes nodded and hurried over.

His Arcane Magic warmed Mae's back as she ran for the exit with Brimstone and Hellreaver. A single thought filled her mind while her sluggish legs carried her up the winding stairs.

Please! Please, don't let me be too late!

NIKOLAI DUCKED BENEATH A DEMON'S SWINGING ARM and narrowly avoided the claws that would have shredded his face. He stabbed the monster in the chest, pressed his foot against the creature's body when it fell to the ground, and tore out his bloodied spear.

A wave of demons and hellbeasts lunged toward him.

Moon Magic and Hellfire Magic heated up his core and lit Alastair's eyes. He raised a hand at them.

"*Moon Fire!*"

Pale flames detonated across the church in a violent boom that consumed the monsters in his path. Their screams of agony made his ears throb as they dropped to the ground and convulsed.

Nikolai panted and straightened, his body tight and his belly quivering with the unholy energy throbbing through him. He felt stronger. Much stronger than he'd ever felt in his entire life. He glanced at the red orb filling the sky through a broken section of roof above him.

Is it because of the Harvest Moon?!

Scarlet drops splattered the pews to his right as Vlad slashed a demon in half and disemboweled another one. Tarang snarled and tore out the throat of a hellwolf.

The incubus glanced at Nikolai, his pupils aglow with demonic energy.

"Go!" he yelled. "You're the only one who can break that altar!"

Nikolai swallowed and bolted toward the chancel. Barquiel cursed where he struggled with Alicia in the vestibule.

Nikolai caught motion out of the corner of his eye. Two hellhounds sprang toward him from the left. *Hell Flare* ate them alive, the heat of the spell so intense it melted the tiles where their charred bodies fell. He skidded to a halt in front of the altar.

Anya Mendes's eerie magic washed across his skin as he gripped his spear.

He scowled at the fiery blue runes licking the obsidian stone, directed his Moon Magic into his weapon, and smashed it down upon the altar.

He didn't make so much as a dent in it.

The blue flames at the base of the obsidian stone flickered.

Nikolai froze. *Did Mae and Cortes free Anya?!*

Frustration churned his stomach as he watched the fire slowly sputter out. The chances that the witch would reverse the spell in time were slim at best. The midnight hour was almost upon them.

I have to shatter the altar!

"Alastair!"

The crow's claws sank deeper into his shoulder.

Nikolai closed his eyes, adrenaline surging through his veins. His blood heated up as he drew on all his magic and that of his familiar. He needed a different spell to break the stone. One more destructive than *Hell Flare* or *Moon Storm*.

His chest tightened. Pale runes flickered into life deep inside his mind. The glowing letters slowly weaved themselves into a fresh conjuration.

Nikolai's eyes slammed open. He took a deep breath, reached for the altar, and opened his mouth to shout out the spell.

Mae's voice reached him a heartbeat before his fingers made contact with the dark stone.

CHAPTER THIRTY-FOUR

M AE'S HEART POUNDED VIOLENTLY AS SHE EMERGED INTO the chancel with Brimstone and Hellreaver. She saw Barquiel force a cursing Alicia inside a portal near the rear of the church and glimpsed the mocking light in the demon's eyes as he glanced at her.

Her gaze found Nikolai. Acid burned the back of her throat.

"Stop!" Mae lunged toward him, her body moving as if her legs were made of treacle. "Don't touch—!"

"RUPTURE!" Nikolai roared.

His head snapped around at the sound of her voice.

Surprise rounded his eyes a second before she collided into him and took him to the ground.

The altar detonated with a sound that made Mae's ears throb. A violent storm erupted inside the church. The blue flames of Anya's magic flickered out as fragments of obsidian stone pelted the interior.

Mae crouched above Nikolai and Alastair. Brimstone shielded them as she raised a barrier to block the debris and a roaring tempest that reeked of magic.

A deafening silence buzzed in her ears when the storm finally abated.

Did I—did I get to him in time?! She swallowed and looked at the man beneath her. *Did he touch the altar?!*

Vlad shouted out her name just as Nikolai blinked his eyes open.

"Nikolai?" Mae mumbled.

He stared at her for moment, his expression blank.

Hate filled his eyes.

No!

The denial tore through her mind at the same time Brimstone's warning rang in her ears.

"My witch!"

Time slowed. Mae was vaguely aware of Nikolai pressing a hand to her belly and Alastair's angry squawk. But she refused to accept what her horrified subconscious was screaming at her. What her eyes were telling her as she met the sorcerer's darkening gaze.

"Moon Spear!"

She gasped and went rigid as the bolt of white magic he'd conjured lanced through her body and tore out of her back. Hot blood drenched her clothes and oozed down his wrist.

Hellreaver arrowed toward Nikolai with a sound of pure fury.

Mae's stomach twisted when the sorcerer caught Hellreaver with his bare hand. He lowered his brows and conjured up another spell, heedless of the serrated blades slashing his palm.

"*Moon Fire!*"

White flames engulfed Hellreaver. Redness bloomed under the pale blaze as the weapon resisted the attack. Mae's heart lurched.

Hellreaver was struggling to fight Nikolai's magic.

Brimstone raised a giant paw to bat away the sorcerer and the angry crow flapping around Mae's head.

"No!" Mae screamed. "*Get away, Brim!*"

Hell Flare engulfed the fox. He flinched amidst the storm of black and red flames, his eyes blazing crimson and his tails making the air vibrate as he endured the devastating effects of the sorcerer's magic.

Nikolai kicked Mae off him.

She landed on her side and skidded several feet across the floor, leaving a trail of blood in her wake. A buzzing filled her skull. She blinked dazedly.

This—this can't be happening!

Crimson slowly pooled beneath her body.

"Mae!" Vlad yelled from across the church. "You bastard! What the hell are you—?!"

The incubus gasped and took Tarang to the ground as Nikolai cast a volley of Hellfire spell bombs at them. One of the attacks scorched Vlad's left shoulder.

Mae bit her lip and swallowed a groan.

Unlike the last time she'd absorbed Nikolai's magic into her body, his power filled her with an agony that scorched her senses. It was as if the loathing she had seen reflected in his eyes now imbued his magic.

I—I need to stop him!

Mae's belly throbbed when she drew on her core. She pressed her hands to the ground, rose shakily onto her knees, and lifted bloodied fingers toward Brimstone and Hellreaver.

"Negate!"

Her heart thundered against her ribs as she watched the spell eat away at *Moon Fire* and *Hell Flare* where they'd almost overwhelmed the fox and the weapon.

Nikolai cursed and rolled onto his feet. He picked up his spear, closed the distance to her, and drove the weapon into her right thigh with a savage snarl.

Mae screamed as it smashed her bone.

Hellreaver screeched. A feral howl tore out of Brimstone and rattled the building.

Vlad's roar of rage echoed in her ears. "MAE!"

The incubus appeared in the chancel.

"Stop!" Mae mumbled. "You can't!" Her voice rose. *"He's too strong!"*

Nikolai ripped the spear out of her flesh, blocked Vlad's swords, and kneed him viciously in the gut. The incubus grunted as he skidded backward, fingers raking the ground to steady himself and a murderous light blazing in his pupils.

Tarang snarled and leapt over a pew to take a bite out of Nikolai's arm. The sorcerer cast *Moon Spear* at the tiger, his face a cold, tight mask.

"Shield!" Mae ground out.

His attack smashed into her barrier and missed the tiger by inches.

Tarang landed on his feet with a thud, bared his fangs at Nikolai, and retreated to Vlad's side.

Mae staggered as she pushed herself up onto her feet, one hand pressed to the wound in her belly. Brimstone and Hellreaver broke free of Nikolai's spells and rushed to her side.

The power of three hummed within her as they reinforced her magic. Crimson bloomed around her body.

The lightning that tore across the sky through the gaping holes in the roof highlighted Nikolai's frosty stare. A cold rain accompanied the peal of thunder that followed. The drops sizzled when they struck the air above her skin.

Cruel laughter drew Mae's gaze to the back of the church. Oscar had reappeared with Drabek. Barquiel stood beside them in Rose's form.

The remaining demons and hellbeasts were disappearing through a portal.

Mae didn't need to analyze Oscar and Barquiel's expressions to know that she'd fully fallen into their trap. All she had to do was look at the hatred in Nikolai's eyes to know they had won this battle. She swallowed.

"You're not thinking clearly right now." Her voice trembled despite her best efforts. Mae clenched her jaw and hardened her tone. "There was another spell hidden in the altar. You triggered it when you touched it." She took a step toward Nikolai, her pulse racing with dread. "Let me help—"

A maniacal bark rooted her legs to the ground.

"Not thinking clearly?!" the sorcerer scoffed. His next words doused any hope she clung to. "That's rich coming from the woman who killed my mother. I'll tell you something now, demon. My mind has never been as clear as it is in this very moment!"

Mae's world tilted sideways.

"What?!" she mumbled. She looked jerkily to Oscar and Rose. Rage tightened her throat when she registered the grim truth in their eyes. "You bastards!"

"Have you lost your fucking mind?!" Vlad shouted at Nikolai. He pointed at Oscar. "The one who killed your mother is right there!"

A vicious expression distorted Nikolai's features. "Keep my brother out of this, you incubus scum!"

Mae's stomach dropped when she read his intent. "SHIELD!"

Her magic bloomed around Vlad and Tarang just as Nikolai cast *Hell Flare* at them.

The sorcerer clenched his jaw and glared at her. He closed the distance to her in the blink of an eye. Mae froze.

Nikolai pressed his hand to her belly and brought his face within a mere whisper of hers even as Brimstone and Hellreaver moved to attack him, his pupils blazing with white fire.

"Subjugate."

CHAPTER THIRTY-FIVE

THE SPELL ROARED THROUGH MAE WITH A VIOLENCE that robbed her of sight and breath. Brimstone and Hellreaver's tortured voices reached her dimly as fire consumed the core of power in her belly.

My witch!

Mae bit the inside of her cheek. Blood flooded her mouth.

Her cry of agony choked off to a ragged moan.

Nikolai's face swam before her eyes. The expression of pure cruelty and loathing he wore as he attempted to undo the red bond that linked her to Brimstone and Hellreaver shattered her heart.

"*Mae!*" Vlad raged. He hammered at the shield still protecting him and Tarang with his fists. "Stop, you crazy bastard!"

Nikolai ignored the incubus. Whiteness flared around his body and that of his crow familiar.

He brought his lips to Mae's ear. "Once this is done, you will be nothing, *demon!*"

Terror knotted Mae's gut. She could feel his magic building up where his fingers scorched her skin. Her consciousness flickered as the ties that bound her to Brimstone and Hellreaver started to waver. She gritted her teeth.

Soul...Shield!...Multiply...Guard!

The spells trembled around her core and those of her familiar and weapon. She didn't know how long they would last in the face of Nikolai's moon-powered magic. Her eyes welled up.

Brimstone and Hellreaver's voices grew even fainter, as did Vlad's desperate shouts. Darkness encroached the edges of her mind.

Is...this...how it ends?! Have I...failed...again?!

A presence Mae hadn't sensed for some time swelled deep within her as her awareness started to fade.

—ae! Mae! WAKE UP MAE!

Mae flinched. *Na—Na Ri?!*

Invoke Purge!

Mae swallowed convulsively, struggling to make sense of her first incarnation's words. *But—we don't possess the necessary white magic to—!*

We do! We have a second core, remember?!

Mae's pulse stuttered.

She gritted her teeth and grabbed on to a semblance of her consciousness. Fire licked her veins as she reached for the power inside her heart. The one she rarely called upon but that Barquiel had attempted to destroy every single time they'd faced one another.

P—Purge!

Incandescent radiance flooded her world on a wave that smelled of Ran Soyun's sweet summer scent. The point of heat that detonated in her chest brought with it Na Ri and their mother's white magic as the spell took form.

Ran Soyun's voice fluttered through her mind. *I can only grant you this power for a brief moment...Use it well, my daughters...This war is far from over...*

Mae's heart swelled. *Thank you, mother!*

Na Ri's voice hardened. *Let's do this, Mae!*

Mae clenched her jaw. A violent detonation boomed around her when they linked their two cores.

Purge started overwriting *Subjugate*.

Nikolai swore and jumped back to a safe distance.

Air wheezed through Mae's throat as she finally drew a breath into her starving lungs. Her bond with Brimstone and Hellreaver reignited with a force that rocked her to the bone and turned the air crimson.

My witch! Brimstone and Hellreaver snarled.

Mae lowered her brows at Nikolai. "This ends now!"

He scowled and raised a Moon Magic shield.

Mae roared as she unleashed the power of three.

Purge destroyed what remained of the sorcerer's spell and swept through the church in a vicious storm that ripped its walls and roof apart.

Wood and bricks pelted Nikolai's barrier. Debris rained down around her.

Mae swayed where she stood before slowly pitching forward. She landed face down in the freezing rain. Her ribcage shuddered violently.

The reality of what had just unfolded pierced her heart and mind, bringing with it a wave of agony that tightened her chest until she could barely breathe. Shallow puddles formed under her broken and battered body, leaching away what little warmth remained in her bones and leaving her veins filled with ice and her throat choked with fear.

A denial fell from her lips in a tortured whisper once more. "No."

The sound was drowned out by the clap of thunder that tore across the distant, angry sky. The ringing echoed in her ears, adding to the dizziness making the world spin around her.

Nausea churned her belly when she attempted to get up. She blinked and bit her lip hard, desperation overriding the despair that threatened to swallow her whole.

Negate! I could try using Negate to overturn the spell!

Fire flared inside her belly as she reached for her magic.

Don't, my witch.

Mae's breath caught at the wretched plea. Tendons screamed in her neck as she turned her head.

Brimstone lay a few feet to her left, his bright eyes and rich fur dulled by the magic attacks they had sustained, his chest quivering with shallow pants. Hellreaver was silent where he poked out from under a pile of rubble next to him, ragged blade gleaming flatly.

Mae clenched her jaw.

Her nails scored the cracked tiles as she garnered the last of her strength and pushed up onto her hands and knees, her limbs trembling so hard she knew she would soon be unable to move. Hotness drenched her abdomen and thigh as blood surged anew from her wounds.

"Stand down, demon," Nikolai said coldly.

Goosebumps prickled her skin at his voice. It took all her willpower to raise her head and meet his gaze.

The sorcerer's mouth was a thin line. He glared at her, his eyes and those of his crow familiar gleaming with distaste. A dark portal distorted the air behind them, the blood-red light of the Harvest Moon adding another layer of menace where it pierced the turbulent clouds visible through the broken church roof.

It framed Oscar and Rose where they stood waiting for him.

Rose laid a hand on Nikolai's arm. "Come. It is time for us to leave."

Fury and anguish curdled Mae's stomach in equal measure at the possessive look the demon gave Nikolai. He nodded curtly, cast a dismissive glance at Mae, and turned to enter the rift.

The tears blurring Mae's vision finally spilled onto her cheeks. "Don't."

His shoulders knotted at her low mumble. For a moment, she thought her voice had finally reached him. The hate that set his pupils aglow when he looked at her shattered whatever slim hope she still clung to.

"You try my patience, demon. Be thankful they asked me to spare you." His gaze swept Oscar and Rose before landing on her once more. "The next time we meet, I will not be as forgiving."

Blood pounded dully in Mae's skull as she watched the three of them disappear inside the rift, disbelief a living thing twisting her insides.

"Don't go!" she begged brokenly.

The portal closed with a hiss of corruption that seemed to mock her.

Mae stared blindly at the spot where Nikolai had vanished, the agony twisting her heart so fierce she almost wished it would strike her dead.

A scrambling sound came behind her.

Vlad climbed the wreckage of broken masonry and wood that was all that remained of the nave and stumbled unsteadily toward her.

"Mae!"

He dropped at her side, his body casting ripples in the growing puddles.

He closed his arms around her and pulled her into his embrace. Mae sagged as his warmth cocooned her. Her fingers dug into his flesh where he cradled her to his chest. Tarang nudged Brimstone and Hellreaver with a worried sound.

A strangled sob finally left her, her throat so tight and hot she struggled to draw air.

"It's okay," Vlad whispered in a harrowed tone. "It's going to be okay."

His trembling voice finally unlocked the scream building up inside her. Mae lifted her face to the stormy sky and bellowed out her rage and loss.

CHAPTER THIRTY-SIX

THE STORM THAT SWEPT THROUGH THE MAGIC community in the aftermath of the Illusion Sorcery the Dark Council had unleashed to make the world turn on Mae and to capture the strongest white magic sorcerer in existence had still not died down a week after the events that had unfolded in the abandoned church outside Concord.

By the time she returned to New York with Vlad, everyone had regained their memories and Mae's status as the country's most wanted fugitive had ended as abruptly as it had begun.

To Mae's relief, it seemed only those with magic in their blood could recall what they had done whilst under the influence of Anya's illusion. Although her family seemed unaware of the week-long fantasy they'd inhabited while under the effect of the spell, she couldn't bring herself to go home. Instead, she spent the days that followed in a daze at Vlad's apartment in Chelsea. She barely remembered him showing her around his place before she'd stumbled into one of his guest rooms and crashed out on the bed.

Alicia came to see her the day after they returned to New York. It had taken the Reaper Queen that long to shatter the prison in which Barquiel had contained her in the Underworld. Though Mae sensed her shock at Nikolai's betrayal, Alicia didn't say anything. They spoke for a short time before she left to take care of her affairs.

From what she'd hinted, there was trouble afoot in Hell.

Mae woke up only to eat the food Vlad brought her, go to the bathroom, and talk briefly with Violet and Miles and her family when they called upon her. She spent the rest of the time hugging Brimstone and Hellreaver to her while they drifted in a dreamless slumber.

There were occasions during the night when she roused briefly to find Vlad sitting quietly by her side, a preoccupied expression on his handsome face as he stared blindly at the cityscape outside the window. He'd healed his left shoulder with his incubus energy. Though only a faint scar remained where Nikolai had burned his flesh, the way he occasionally touched the wound told Mae it still bothered him.

An unexpected visitor turned up on the sixth day.

Mae had just crawled back into bed when a distant yipping reached her ears. She burrowed under the sheets, tugged Brimstone and Hellreaver to her chest, and started dozing off again.

The yipping got louder.

"I didn't know tigers yipped," Mae mumbled.

They don't, Brimstone murmured. *That's Dexter.*

Mae stiffened. "As in Mrs. Son-Ha's Chihuahua?"

The door slammed open. A ball of fur bolted across the room, jumped onto Mae's stomach with enough force to make her wheeze, and worked its way under the sheets.

Dexter's tail blurred as he licked her face with aggressive enthusiasm. His owner marched inside the bedroom.

"You should air this place," Mrs. Son-Ha stated sourly as she looked around.

"We shouldn't disturb her," Vlad protested, trailing in her wake.

"She's had enough rest." Mrs. Son-Ha stopped by the bed and put her hands on her hips with the expression of a drill sergeant about to tear into a soldier. "Get up."

"Don't wanna," Mae said sullenly.

The old woman yanked the sheets off her. Mae sucked in air and backpedaled until she was sitting against the headboard, Brimstone and Hellreaver clutched defensively to her chest.

Mrs. Son-Ha pointed imperiously at the bathroom. "You stink. Go shower. Now!"

Mae scowled.

"Don't make me take you in there and scrub you down," Mrs. Son-Ha threatened.

Mae glared at her before climbing off the bed and storming into the bathroom. She slammed the door shut. It opened again.

Mrs. Son-Ha dumped Brimstone and Hellreaver unceremoniously inside. "They need a wash too." She directed a narrow-eyed look at Vlad over her shoulder. "You, go make breakfast."

"Yes, ma'am," the incubus mumbled.

Mae glowered at the door when it shut again. She hesitated, stripped out of the nightshirt Violet had brought over from her apartment, and got under the shower.

"Cortes was right," she grumbled, squirting soap into her hands and lathering up Brimstone and Hellreaver. "She should be a cartel leader."

The fox sneezed as bubbles got into his nose.

Mae emerged from the guest room a while later. The smell of freshly roasted coffee made her stomach growl when she crossed the landing. She headed down the stairs spiraling to the first floor of Vlad's penthouse and made her way to the kitchen.

Her right leg twinged a little, courtesy of the wound Nikolai had inflicted on her. Her broken bone and the hole in her abdomen had healed the night she'd incurred the injuries. All that remained was an ache that would soon fade.

She wished the pain in her heart would abate as easily.

The juicer came to life just as she entered the kitchen.

Mae rocked to a halt and eyed the green liquid in the machine Vlad was operating. "Please tell me that's not breakfast."

Vlad switched it off with a grimace. "It's for Mrs. Son-Ha."

The subject of their conversation strolled in. She beamed at the sight of him pouring the contents into a glass.

"This is a nice place you have here." The old woman climbed onto a stool at the breakfast bar and accepted the drink. "My spirits approve."

"Thank you," Vlad said grudgingly.

He handed Mae a cup of coffee and took out sausages, eggs, and bacon from the refrigerator. Tarang trotted into the kitchen just as the incubus put three platters of assorted, raw meat in his breakfast spot. The tiger licked his chops, came over to nudge Brimstone and Hellreaver, and headed over to his meal. The fox and the weapon hesitated before following him.

Mae bit her lip. She knew they hated leaving her side even for a moment. The ordeal they had suffered still haunted them. If it hadn't been for her second core and Ran Soyun's magic, *Subjugate* would have worked.

It wasn't until they'd finished breakfast that Mrs. Son-Ha voiced what she'd come to say.

"Take heart. The future is not set in stone. You can still save him."

Mae stiffened and met Vlad's troubled gaze. Right now, neither of them could see a light at the end of that particular tunnel.

She knew the incubus had spent days racking his brain to figure out how they could free Nikolai from the Dark Council's influence, just as she had done in the hours when she'd been awake.

Mae recalled what Mrs. Son-Ha had told them the night they'd discovered she was a Shaman. "Was Nikolai turning against me one of the outcomes you foresaw?"

Vlad lowered his brows at her question.

"It was the most likely one." Mrs. Son-Ha hesitated at Mae's frustrated stare. "But warning you about it would have cast ripples in your destiny that would have had unintended consequences."

Mae's hands bunched on her lap. "You mean, things could have been worse?"

Mrs. Son-Ha ignored her shrill tone. She leaned over and laid a gentle hand on Mae's knuckles.

"Your death was one of the futures I divined," she said quietly.

Vlad paled. Brimstone and Hellreaver whined and hastily returned to her side, their distress at the old woman's words resonating across their bond with her.

"I would never want that to happen, Mae," Mrs. Son-Ha continued in a kind voice. "Not just because I care for you like I would my own daughter. But because the world needs you."

Mae swallowed, the burden of the destiny Bryony had told her of the day they'd met weighing her down with invisible shackles once more. For a moment, she wished she wasn't the Witch Queen. That she'd carried on living her life blissfully unaware of the world of magic and the otherworldly reality that existed around her.

But then I wouldn't have met Brimstone and Hellreaver and Vlad, and everyone else I've come to cherish in the last year. She caressed the fox and the weapon as they huddled against her, emotion choking her breath. *And I wouldn't have fallen in love with Nikolai.*

Mrs. Son-Ha's expression hardened. "You know what you have to do."

CHAPTER THIRTY-SEVEN

THE NOISE LEVEL INSIDE THE MAIN FOYER OF THE headquarters of the New York coven faded to a tense hush when Mae entered the building with Violet and Miles.

A sea of awkward stares landed on them.

Mae clenched her jaw. It was her first visit to the coven since they'd turned on her. She started across the lobby, determined to get this done and over with. The crowd of sorcerers and witches parted hastily ahead of her.

"This is worse than Uncle Ernest's funeral," Violet muttered.

"You obviously missed what happened between Regina and Aunt Constance in the kitchen at Uncle Joseph's funeral," Miles said sourly.

Violet grimaced. "Why, did they fight?"

"Worse. Regina told Aunt Constance her fish pie was a dud." Miles shuddered. "Erik looked like he was gonna have a fit. If Aunt Barbara hadn't been there, it would have been handbags at dawn."

He cleared his throat and gave Mae a sidelong glance.

Mae swallowed a sigh. Even though she'd come out of Vlad's guest room, everyone was still walking on eggshells around her. It was as if they'd all decided she'd break if they said or did the wrong thing.

A low growl reached her. She looked at Brimstone.

The fox was wearing a menacing expression where he padded beside her, his tail brushing against her leg. He still hadn't forgiven the coven for what they'd done to them.

Their stares are making me twitchy, my witch. Hellreaver trembled on her chest. *My blades are demanding payback.*

A little slash and a nip won't hurt them too much, Brimstone grunted.

"Stop it, you two," Mae chided. "You know they weren't in their right minds when they attacked us."

We could plead temporary insanity after we cut them, Hellreaver suggested.

Violet observed the red haze fluttering around Brimstone and the weapon warily. "Are they being bloodthirsty again?"

"You don't know the half of it," Mae muttered.

The sorcerer manning the reception desk on the top floor froze when they emerged from the elevator. The coven members sitting in the waiting area straightened, the color draining from their faces.

Brent Perkins shot out of his chair and bowed reverentially at the waist.

"Witch Queen," he greeted in a quavering voice.

A frog popped his head out of his pocket and issued a penitent croak.

"Hi, Brent." Mae made a face. "How about you go back to calling me Mae, like before?"

"I—I cannot do that, my queen," Brent quavered. "We owe you our deepest apologies!"

This is driving me crazy. Mae rubbed the back of her neck. *We can't go on like this.*

I don't know, Brimstone growled. *I quite like the way they're groveling.*

"Look, it's all water under the—" Mae started.

She flinched when the witch who'd been in the waiting area jumped up and rushed over to prostrate herself before her.

"I'm so sorry, Witch Queen!" the woman cried wretchedly. "I was wrong to attack you! Please, punish me as you see fit!"

Her dog whined and dropped down beside her.

It took a second for Mae to recognize the witch who'd been manning the reception the night she and Nikolai had returned to New York and discovered the effects of the magic she had triggered in the church on Marblehead Neck.

"This is going great, by the way," Violet observed drily.

Mae cut her eyes to her.

Violet shrugged. "I mean, it's better than them throwing spell bombs at us."

Brent's chin wobbled. The witch on the floor whimpered.

Miles groaned at his cousin. "Did you have to put it that way?"

The pair started bickering with one another.

Mae sighed. *At least they're starting to act normal.*

She leaned down and extended a hand toward the witch lying prone on the floor.

"Honestly, it's—*whoa!*"

She jerked back as the three sorcerers in the waiting area fell to their knees and crawled toward her with various pleas of "Please forgive us!" and "Please, punish us, Witch Queen!"

"Looks like you started a new religion," Violet said unhelpfully.

I call dibs on that witch, Hellreaver declared.

Brimstone glared at the dog. *That pup won't be able to procreate after I'm done with him.*

Mae scowled at everyone.

"What's going on?" someone said briskly.

She looked around. Abraham was coming down the corridor.

Mae raked her hair with her fingers. "You tell me."

Abraham narrowed his eyes at the recumbent witch and sorcerers in the reception. "I'm pretty sure Bryony told you guys to treat her as if nothing had happened."

Brent straightened. "But—but we've wronged her!"

The witch on the ground nodded numbly.

Abraham's lip curled. "If she was still upset about it, we'd be standing in a crater right now."

The witch and the sorcerers paled.

"I'm not that reckless," Mae protested.

"We both know that's a lie." Abraham's expression softened at her frown. "Come, the others are waiting."

He led the way to the conference chamber.

Mae frowned as she followed the sorcerer. One week later and the New York coven's horror at their own betrayal had still not faded. She wasn't sure if that scar would ever truly heal.

Yet another reason to pummel Vedran's face when we finally find him.

Indeed, Brimstone huffed.

Bryony rose self-consciously when Mae entered her office. The rest of the High Council stilled where they sat and stood in their respective chambers on the video display on the wall.

"Hi, Mae," Raven Quinn said in a strained voice.

The High Priestess of the L.A. coven was one of the few people who hadn't fallen under the spell of Anya Mendes's Illusion Sorcery, along with Derrick Adlington and Karin Everheart, the heads of the Baton Rouge and San Francisco covens. They'd been out of the country at the time.

"Hey," Mae greeted her.

Brimstone and Hellreaver ignored everyone and shot across the room to a cart stacked with trays of steak.

She narrowed her eyes. "How about you two say thank you for the food?"

A sullen *Yeah, thanks* rose from the familiar and the weapon as they stuffed their faces without looking at anyone.

Bryony pushed a tray of sandwiches across her desk as Mae took the seat opposite her. "There's extra pastrami and mustard in those."

Mae nodded. A fraught hush ensued.

She swallowed a sigh. *God, I hate this tension between us.*

She was debating how to break the awkward silence when a crunching sound came from behind her. She looked over her shoulder.

Miles froze when he became the focus of their stares, his mouth full of the BLT he'd just bitten into.

He chewed and swallowed nervously. "What? I skipped lunch."

Mae's stomach grumbled.

Everyone relaxed as she helped herself to a pastrami sandwich. She was halfway through it when she realized everyone was still staring at her.

Mae grimaced and licked her lips. "Have I got something on my face?"

Violet sighed. Miles stiffened guiltily where he was attempting to swipe another sandwich from the tray.

Ephra Erwin pinched the bridge of her nose. "We're kind of waiting for you to tell us off."

"Oh." Mae exchanged a glance with Violet and Miles. They dipped their heads slightly. "So, yeah, how about we put all of that behind us?"

Bryony drew a sharp breath. Even Abraham looked stunned at her words.

Karen frowned. "We can't just ignore what happened, Mae. The repercussions of the entire magic community betraying the Witch Queen is being felt not just in this country, but all over the world!"

"And that's exactly what Vedran wants."

Her words made them stiffen.

"Spreading discord and strife is how he works," Mae continued, trying her best to keep the bitterness out of her voice. "Besides, there's something you all seem to be forgetting."

"What?" Abraham asked stiltedly.

"Apart from those who possess Arcane Magic, demonic power, or divine protection, no one was immune to Anya Mendes's Illusion Sorcery. Not even —" Mae faltered and looked at her hands before raising her head and meeting their stricken stares unflinchingly, "not even Nikolai could fight that spell in the end."

"You're right," Bryony said after a tense lull. "Arguing about why we fell for that illusion won't help us do what we need to do next."

Ephra nodded briskly. "We have to find where they're hiding Stanisic."

"No."

Mae's voice echoed around Bryony's office.

She saw Violet and Miles trade a troubled glance out of the corner of her eye. They'd argued with her at length when she'd told them her intentions.

A muscle jumped in Abraham's cheek. "What do you mean, no? We have to save Nikolai!"

"*I* will save him," Mae said quietly.

Horrified realization dawned in their eyes at her

words. Her gut twisted. The look on Nikolai's face when she'd last seen him hardened her resolve.

This is for the best. It has *to be this way. For now.*

Bryony swallowed, her expression pained. "Is it because you can't trust us anymore?"

"It's because I don't have a way to fight Illusion Sorcery yet."

Abraham flinched. Confusion washed across the High Council's faces.

"Anya Mendes and Gloria Espenoza believe there are a handful of others in the world who wield their magic," Mae explained in a hard voice. "According to Sergio Mendes and Enrique Cortes's coven, there have been rumors of Arcane Magic users in China and in Africa. Where there is Arcane Magic, Illusion Sorcery may follow."

Bryony's shoulders knotted.

Mae masked a sad smile when she saw understanding darken the older woman's eyes. She knew the witch would get her meaning first.

"So, what you're saying is you don't want to take the risk of the Dark Council using that spell against us a second time?" Bryony mumbled.

Mae nodded. "As much as I hate having to take them on without your help, I don't want to jeopardize Nikolai's rescue."

Abraham fisted his hands, his frustration mirrored on the faces of the High Council. "If Vedran unleashes that spell again and we tattle, your plans are screwed, is that it?"

"Pretty much." Mae sighed ruefully at their wretched glares. "Look, I'd really hate to have to hurt you all."

"You seemed to be enjoying hurting me plenty on Staten Island," Abraham grumbled.

Mae made a face. "That's because you turned into a total asshole under that spell."

Abraham accepted this statement grudgingly.

"It won't be for long," she promised. "I just need to

figure out a way to protect everyone's minds against Illusion Sorcery."

Bryony glanced at Violet and Miles. "They'll be helping you?"

Mae dipped her chin. "Along with Vlad. And Alicia, hopefully."

Unease prickled her skin. It had been over a week since she'd last seen the Reaper Queen.

Karin's voice brought her attention back to the current discussion.

"Just the five of you, against the entire Dark Council?" the witch said harshly. "That's madness!"

"No," Derrick observed with a brooding look. "It might just work. A small team will be inconspicuous."

Raven frowned. "I still think they need some help."

They talked for a while longer before ending the meeting.

Mae parted ways with Violet and Miles outside the coven headquarters and headed to her family's home in Flushing. She'd promised them she'd come over for dinner tonight. With Nikolai gone, her apartment felt empty. It also held too many painful memories for Mae, even though they'd only lived together since summer.

Vlad had suggested she move in with him.

Mae hadn't been sure what to make of the incubus's proposal and had asked for some time to think it over. To her surprise, neither Brimstone nor Hellreaver had teased her on the subject. She got the feeling they quite liked having Vlad and Tarang around.

Mae turned her Vespa into her street and slowed.

There were two SUVs parked outside her house. A familiar magic brushed across her skin as she drew level with them.

I can smell Popo, Brimstone said from the basket.

Mae spotted Noah Tegner's men watching the Medellin coven sorcerers guardedly while they patrolled the area around the property. A different magic flittered against her core and made her frown. She rolled her scooter onto the driveway and headed inside, curious as to why her other visitors were here.

Ye-Seul was taking a plate of sweet rice cakes out of the refrigerator when Mae strolled into the kitchen. Yoo-Mi was washing a cabbage at the sink.

Anya Mendes and her father put down their cups of tea hastily and rose.

"Hello," Anya greeted her solemnly.

Mendes bowed stiffly. "Witch Queen."

"Er, hi." Mae studied Anya closely. It was her first time seeing the witch since she and Cortes had dropped by Vlad's apartment in the days following their return to New York. "Your wounds look better."

A sad smile curved the witch's mouth. "Valentina Flores left a healer with us before she returned to Caracas."

Ye-Seul paused in the act of serving their guests rice cake. "I smell pastrami and mustard."

Mae rolled her eyes. "I had lunch at the coven." She pulled out a chair. "Where's Ryu?"

"Out shopping with Noah."

Mendes squared his shoulders. "We've come to offer our official apology, Witch Queen. Our coven will pay the city reparations for the damages incurred at the hotel where the reception was held. We—"

He faltered and stopped. His hare made a soft sound at his feet.

Anya clasped Mendes's hand.

He looked gratefully at his daughter and fixed Mae with a determined stare. "We hope to continue to serve you to our best capacity."

Mae wrinkled her nose. "How about you stay for dinner?"

"I already asked," Yoo-Mi said briskly. "We're having *bibimbap* and *bulgogi*." She glanced at Brimstone and Hellreaver. "I take it the meat eaters want steak?"

Brimstone's ears perked up. Hellreaver hummed.

"They had steak for lunch." Mae ignored the fox and the weapon's protests. "They'll have what we're having."

The pair drooped.

Mae cut her eyes to the parrot perched next to the harpy eagle on the kitchen counter. "Where's your lord and master?"

"I'm behind you."

Mae jumped and clutched her chest with a hand before whirling around. "Jesus, has anyone ever told you that you walk like a cat?!"

"A number of people," Cortes drawled. "Right before I killed them."

Ye-Seul sucked in air, her face brightening with barely concealed glee at this admission. Yoo-Mi shot a narrow-eyed look at the Columbian.

"Sorry." Cortes took the seat next to Mae. "How are you doing?"

"I'm good," Mae grunted. "In fact, I'm itching to kick the Dark Council's ass."

Surprise flared on Cortes and the Mendes' faces.

"You have a plan of action?" Cortes asked in a hard voice.

Mae's shoulders slumped. "Not quite."

She chewed her lip and pinned Anya and Cortes with a shrewd look.

"What is it?" the witch said curiously.

"I want the two of you to teach me how to counter Illusion Sorcery."

Anya's eyes widened. Cortes stared. Mendes gaped.

Mae told them what she'd said to the New York coven.

Understanding dawned on Anya's face. "You want to make sure your friends never turn on you again?"

Mae stole a glance at Ye-Seul and Yoo-Mi. "Not just my friends."

Anya's expression grew strained.

Mae grimaced. "Look, I can't fight the Dark Council on my own. I need the entire magic community to help me. But if Vedran succeeds in turning me into your enemy again, he *will* be the victor of this war."

"No one except those who possess Arcane Magic has ever successfully deflected an Illusion Sorcery spell," Mendes said in a troubled voice. "Even if you were able to do it, to spread that magic on the scale you're suggesting would be impossible."

Mae watched him steadily. "Would it be impossible for someone with two cores?"

Mendes recoiled. Anya gasped. Cortes froze.

"What, is two cores special or something?" Ye-Seul asked curiously.

"Yes," Cortes murmured.

Mae sighed at the Columbian's leery expression. "Look, I don't particularly want to shout that fact from the rooftop. Barquiel is the only other person who seems to know I have two cores."

Anya swallowed and glanced at her father. "I—in that case, what you're suggesting is worth trying."

Mendes hesitated before dipping his head. Cortes lowered his brows.

"Would it pose a danger to Anya?" he asked Mae in clipped tones.

She blinked. "I don't think so."

Cortes seemed relieved at that. He brought his cup to his lips.

Ye-Seul turned to Anya. "By the way, is your eagle dating his parrot?"

Anya choked on a rice cake. Cortes swallowed his tea down the wrong pipe. Yoo-Mi's eyes bulged.

Ye-Seul indicated the evidence before their eyes. "I mean, he keeps giving her his nuts."

Popo froze in the act of passing some of his food to Sable.

Yoo-Mi looked at the ceiling.

"How am I even related to her?" she mumbled to an unseen deity.

Mae smirked when she saw Anya's flushed ears and

the coy glance the witch shot at Cortes. She leaned sideways toward the coughing sorcerer while an oblivious Mendes passed his daughter some tea. "So, you and Anya, huh?"

Cortes's expression turned frosty as he wiped his mouth. "I don't know what you mean."

Mae's grin widened at the obvious lie. She poked him in the ribs with an elbow and ignored his wince.

"You sly dog, you. Wait till I tell Vlad."

Cortes glowered at her.

THE END

Mae, Brimstone, and Hellreaver's adventures continue in A Fury of Shadows, the penultimate book in the Witch Queen series.

ACKNOWLEDGMENTS

To my friends and family. I couldn't do this without you.

To my readers. Thank you for reading Midnight Witch. If you enjoyed my book, please consider leaving a review on Goodreads or on the store where you purchased it. Reviews help readers like you find my books and I truly appreciate your honest opinions about my stories.

Make sure to sign up to my store newsletter for special deals on my books and new release alerts. Or you can sign up to my author newsletter to get upcoming release notifications, sneak peeks, and giveaways.

BOOKS BY A.D. STARRLING

Legion

ABOUT A.D. STARRLING

Visit Shop AD Starrling and buy all of AD's ebooks, paperbacks, hardbacks, audiobooks, and exclusive special edition print books direct.

Want to know about AD Starrling's upcoming releases? Sign up to her author newsletter for new release alerts, sneak peeks, giveaways, and more.

Follow AD Starrling on Amazon.

Join AD's reader group on Facebook
The Seventeen Club.

Check out this link to find out more about A.D. Starrling
Linktr.ee/AD_Starrling.